CAMPBELL'S
WEATHER COMPENDIUM

Harry Campbell

PORTICO

You don't need a weatherman to know
which way the wind blows.

Bob Dylan

INTRODUCTION

The weather is always with us, and all around us. It links us in a unique way to the past and to unfamiliar places. Turner painted the same clouds we know today: when we look into one of his skies we lose all sense of the gulf of time that separates us from the artist. The same clouds have been a trigger to the imagination of poets and dreamers on one hand, and classified and checked off lists by cloud-spotting enthusiasts on the other.

In Britain, whatever the state of the economy, we are rich in weather. There are places in the world where there is no significant change in the weather for weeks or months or even years, places which don't even have seasons, only a climate; but in the dear old British Isles the weather can sometimes give the impression of never staying the same an hour at a time. If you don't like the weather here, visitors to Scotland are told, just wait 15 minutes. You can experience four seasons in one day.

We love to complain about the weather, it is a classic British pastime, but there are worse crosses to bear. Not only are we rarely bored, the more unpredictable the climate, the more we appreciate good weather when it comes. The exhilaration of waking up to a glorious sunny day, of stepping out into the smiling warmth of summer with white clouds scudding cheerfully overhead, is surely lost on those living in places where every day is a sunny day. Everywhere looks better when the weather is fine, the world generally seems like a less grim place – that somehow seems like a universal truth, but perhaps it's stronger among those who can't take sunshine for granted. Certainly there's an extra joy in being on holiday in an unreliable climate, and finding that your act of faith has been rewarded by the smiling heavens.

Meteorology is a highly complex science, and not the most exact. Even today with all the high-tech apparatus at the forecaster's command – satellites, radar, computer simulations – the holy grail of the straightforward, comprehensible, reliable weather forecast still seems a long way off. The ordinary person still struggles to fathom the secrets of the weather. Thus it is that the wealth of folklore and mythology surrounding the subject has hardly lost its power: our forefathers devised a thousand homely rhymes and maxims and many of them are still current today. The names of scientists of all nationalities are preserved in the effects, processes and phenomena they bequeathed to the world, from Hadley cells to the Coriolis effect to the splendidly named Madden-Julian oscillation.

The language of the weather is a delight. On the one hand we have quaint old country expressions, on the other a complex cosmopolitan web of nomenclature. Often words for specific phenomena are imported from their country of origin (Harmattan, Föhn wind, el Niño), and even provide model names for the motor industry (Sirocco). Charmingly evocative terms like mackerel sky and mares' tails contrast with the systematic Latinate structures devised to describe and categorise clouds (cumulonimbus, cirrostratus and so on). You can tick them off like a cloud spotter, or lie on your back staring up at them and sigh like Baudelaire about 'les nuages qui passent!' (Or, come to that, you can stare at trails of condensation left by aeroplanes and imagine a conspiracy to dose the world with 'chemicals'.)

But the weather is serious business too. It has a huge impact on the economy and hence on human history. The dust bowls of the American prairie in the 1930s were an ecological and human disaster with lasting consequences, and many are the examples of the course of human history being changed when weather takes a hand in wartime, from the Spanish Armada to the oft-told story of the tin buttons on Napoleonic uniforms that crumbled in the cold of the Russian winter.

Today we see its sheer destructive power with ever-increasing frequency, according to the doomsayers. Whether the weather is actually getting 'worse' is a matter of scientific debate, but to think so appeals to the pessimism in many of us. What is certainly true is that the images of hurricanes and floods are more in our eyes in the age of shocking television reports from all over the world. Natural weather disasters have always happened, from Bangladesh to Boscastle, though we didn't always see what they looked like from helicopters filming directly over them. In recent years, we have become complacent about dangers that have existed for centuries and which have been exacerbated by the nature of our built environment, with hard paved and metalled surfaces and more and more demand for building land where no houses should have been put.

Despite both a highly developed understanding of the science behind it and a vastly improved ability to predict it, what has not changed is our own powerlessness in the face of extreme weather. After unsatisfactory experiments in the 20th century, notably by means of cloud seeding to produce rain, and dark rumours of lives lost in manmade flooding, the British authorities have largely given up trying to modify the weather. However, such attempts have not altogether ceased: it is said that in China there are more people working on controlling the weather than on predicting it.

It is perhaps a bitter irony that, while attempts to bend the weather to our will have largely failed, we have been all too accidentally successful in changing the world's weather. Stories of manmade environmental disasters go back throughout history, but never on the scale of the present day, where few respectable authorities now contest the gradual warming effect caused by both the industrial and agricultural revolutions, a by-product of the sheer scale of human settlement and increasing affluence around the world, to which we have been blind for too long. The release into the atmosphere of greenhouse gases such as carbon dioxide and methane has had a subtle but massively significant effect on climate patterns, and, while we may only just be starting to see the effects, they will have very far-reaching consequences indeed.

White Christmas
(just like the ones I used to know)

Despite its iconic status in the imagery of Christmas, snow rarely falls on Christmas Day in the UK nowadays. All it takes to win a bet on a white Christmas occurring is for a single snowflake to be observed falling at some point during the 24 hours of 25 December, yet the festive punter is nearly always disappointed.

In previous centuries, white Christmases were more common, for various reasons. Britain's climate is warmer today than it was even 200 years ago, when we were emerging from the grip of the Little Ice Age of 1550–1850, when the Thames would sometimes freeze over. Snow is more likely in the New Year than late December, and this effect was increased by the change in the calendar that took place in 1752, when Britain moved from the Julian to the Gregorian system, which effectively brought Christmas Day back by 12 days.

In Britain, your best chance of spotting a festive snowflake is not on the roof of the Met Office in London, where only 13% of Christmases since 1950 have been white, but in the north-east of Scotland: Aberdeen has had one every four years on average, and Lerwick has done even better with nearly one white Christmas in three. A notable exception was 2004, with snow covering Scotland and Northern Ireland as well as much of Wales, the Midlands, north-east and south-west England.

❄ ❄ ❄

Weather Cocktails: Part I

Sea Breeze   Vodka, cranberry juice and grapefruit juice.

Dark and Stormy   Dark rum and ginger beer over ice.

Hurricane   Rum, lime juice and passion-fruit syrup.

Sundowner   Malibu, pineapple juice and Angostura bitters.

Tequila Sunrise   Tequila, orange juice and grenadine (or tequila, crème de cassis, lime juice and soda water).

Red Sea Sunrise   Lemonade, orange juice and grenadine.

❈ ❈ ❈

Fair Weather Fact

Lightning is five times hotter than the surface of the sun.

❈ ❈ ❈

Rain: A Story in Song

The word 'rain' has been an obsessive reference for songwriters. 'I Wish it Would Rain,' sighed The Temptations in 1967. 'Dusty' Springfield, just a year later, was optimistic about the chances of some much-needed moisture: 'I Think it's Gonna Rain Today'. 'A Hard Rain's A-gonna Fall,' agreed grumpy old curmudgeon Bob Dylan. 'More Than Rain,' said Tom Waits cryptically. 'Red Rain,' suggested the White Stripes, even more cryptically. 'Purple Rain,' corrected the artist still known in 1984 as Prince. The Ink Spots, and Ella Fitzgerald, attempted to restore clam with a philosophical nugget. 'Into Each Life Some Rain Must Fall,' they said consolingly, quoting Longfellow. But 'Why Does it Always Rain on Me?' whinged miserabilists Travis in their breakthrough single of 1999. Well, if you will live in Glasgow, you're bound to spend some time 'Walking in the Rain' to quote the Ronettes, as Barry White did, not to mention Grace Jones on the 1981 album *Nightclubbing*. 'Singin' in the Rain,' maybe – Gene Kelly was ever the optimist – or maybe 'Crying in the Rain' like those sensitive Everly Brothers 10 years later in 1962. But it took Mahalia Jackson, and indeed Sister Rosetta Tharpe, to hammer home the point: 'Didn't it Rain?' Well, yes indeed, sisters, of that there can be no doubt.

❋ ❋ ❋

Well Said...

When two Englishmen meet,
their first talk is of the weather.
Samuel Johnson

❈ ❈ ❈

The Beaufort Scale

The Beaufort Wind Force Scale (see next page) was devised in 1806 by Sir Francis Beaufort, an admiral in the British Royal Navy. He is said to have become a hydrographer (someone who studies oceans, seas, rivers and lakes) after having been shipwrecked as a child thanks to a defective sea-chart. His scale is used today (with slight variations) all over the world. Before its adoption, though, observing and recording the weather was a standard part of a naval officer's activities, there was no standard way of describing wind strengths.

In the 1940s, Forces 13 to 17 were added for use in China, to cater for tropical cyclones. The Saffir-Simpson Hurricane Scale, invented in the 1970s, dovetails with the Beaufort Scale and theoretically connects to the system of Mach numbers, which relate to the speed of sound, while tornadoes are measured on the Enhanced Fujita Scale.

Force	Wind speed (knots, mph, km/h)	Description	On land	At sea (wave heights in open water, not onshore)
O	0–1, 0–1, 0–1.6	Calm	Smoke rises vertically	Flat calm
1	1–3, 1–3, 1.6–4.8	Light Air	Smoke drifts in wind direction, wind vanes do not move	Sea shows tiny ripples
2	4–6, 4–7, 6.4–11.3	Light Breeze	Leaves rustle, wind felt on face, wind vanes move	Small non-breaking wavelets
3	7–10, 8–12, 12.9–19.3	Gentle breeze	Twigs move, small flags fly	Large wavelets (1–3ft/31–91cm) with breaking crests
4	11–16, 13–18, 21–29	Moderate breeze	Small branches move, dust blows about	Small waves (3–6ft/1–1.8m) with 'white horses' ('whitecaps')
5	17–21, 19–24, 30.6–38.6	Fresh breeze	Small trees move	Moderate waves (6–8ft/1.8–2.4m), many white horses, some spray
6	22–27, 25–31, 40.2–50	Strong breeze	Large branches move, overhead wires whistle, difficult to use umbrella	Large waves (8–13ft/2.4–4m) with crests
7	28–33, 32–38, 51.5–61.2	High wind, near gale	Whole trees move, resistance felt when walking	Breaking waves (13–20ft/4–6m) with white foam blows in streaks
8	34–40, 39–46, 62.8–74	Gale	Small branches break off, hard to walk	Waves 20–25ft/6–7.6m, spindrift and foam in streaks
9	41–47, 47–54, 75.6–87	Strong gale, severe gale	Slight structural damage (chimney pots and slates)	High waves (25–30ft/7.6–9.1m) with tumbling crests, dense foam, spray affects visibility
10	48–55, 55–63, 88.5–101.4	Storm, whole gale	Trees uprooted, buildings damaged	Very high waves (30–40ft/9.1–12.2m), with curling overhanging crests, heavy rolling
11	56–63, 64–73, 103–117.5	Violent storm, severe storm	Widespread damage (rare on land)	Extremely high waves (40–50ft/12.2–15.2m), foam covers sea
12	63+, 74+, 119+	Hurricane force	Wholesale destruction (very rare)	Waves over 45ft (13.7m), sea white with foam, air full of spray.

Record Weather: Hottest

The highest temperature ever recorded was at Al'Aziziyah in Libya at 57.8°C (136°F) on 13 September 1922. The hottest annual average belongs to Dallal, Ethiopia, which between 1960 and 1966 averaged 34.4°C (94°F).

※ ※ ※

Coup de Foudre

That's what the French call it when you fall in love at first sight: the lightning strike. It's a particularly unfortunate image for those who have experienced a real lightning strike, especially given a recent story from Tennessee. In June 2010 a 25-year-old Knoxville woman called Bethany Lott was fatally struck while she and her boyfriend, Richard Butler, were visiting a mountainous beauty spot called Max Patch Bald. There had been a storm, but the rain had stopped and all seemed normal. 'God, baby, look how beautiful it is,' she said to him, seconds before the lightning struck. He was also hit, but survived. 'I was spun 180 degrees and thrown several feet back,' he said. 'My legs turned to Jell-O [jelly], my shoes were smoking and the bottom of my feet felt like they were on fire.' A tragic enough occurrence by any measure, but especially poignant on this occasion: Butler had brought an engagement ring with him. He had been just about to propose.

※ ※ ※

When to Visit ... Sydney

December
Av. daily sunshine: 8 hrs
Av. monthly rainfall: 3in (74mm)
Av. max. temperature: 25°C (77°F)

❋ ❋ ❋

Fair Weather Fact

A rainbow was visible for six hours in Wetherby, Yorkshire, on 14 March 1994. This is incredibly rare as most rainbows last for only a few minutes.

❋ ❋ ❋

Postcards From Far Away

A postcard home:

The weather is here.
Wish you were beautiful.

❋ ❋ ❋

Not-very-Musical Instruments

Link these weather instruments with their occupation:

1. Barometer
2. Thermometer
3. Psychometer
4. Anemometer
5. Wind vane/sock
6. Weather balloon
7. Weather satellite
8. Rain gauge
9. Campbell Stokes Recorder

a. Measures wind direction
b. Measures sunshine
c. Measures weather in higher atmospheres
d. Measures air pressure
e. Measures rain and snow
f. Measures relative humidity
g. Measures wind speed
h. Measures air temperature
i. Photographs and tracks large movements of air

Answers on p.164

❀   ❀   ❀

Hollywood Weather

Blockbuster movies that *sound* as if they might be about the weather:

- *Gone With the Wind* (1939)
- *Sunset Boulevard* (1950)
- *Singin' in the Rain* (1952)
- *The Sun Also Rises* (1957)
- *Some Like It Hot* (1959)
- *Dog Day Afternoon* (1975)
- *An Autumn Afternoon* (1962)
- *Endless Summer* (1966)
- *A Man for All Seasons* (1966)
- *Finian's Rainbow* (1968)
- *The Lion in Winter* (1968)
- *Brewster McCloud* (1970)
- *Autumn Sonata* (1978)
- *The Shining* (1980)
- *The Big Chill* (1983)
- *St. Elmo's Fire* (1985)
- *Under the Cherry Moon* (1986)
- *One Crazy Summer* (1986)
- *Empire of the Sun* (1987)
- *Gorillas in the Mist* (1988)
- *Tequila Sunrise* (1988)
- *Rain Man* (1988)
- *Days of Thunder* (1990)
- *Cool Runnings* (1993)
- *My Favourite Season* (1993)
- *Waterworld* (1995)
- *Heat* (1995)
- *From Dusk till Dawn* (1996)
- *Twister* (1996)
- *White Squall* (1996)
- *The Fifth Element* (1997)
- *The Ice Storm* (1997)
- *Hard Rain* (1998)
- *If the Sun Rises in the West* (1998)
- *The Waterboy* (1998)
- *Blow* (2001)
- *Vanilla Sky* (2001)
- *The Perfect Storm* (2001)
- *Gathering Storm* (2002)
- *Ice Age* (2002)
- *Eternal Sunshine of the Spotless Mind* (2004)
- *The Weather Man* (2005)
- *Little Miss Sunshine* (2006)
- *Stormbreaker* (2006)
- *The Wind That Shakes the Barley* (2006)
- *The Mist* (2007)
- *Frozen River* (2008)
- *500 Days of Summer* (2009)
- *Cloudy With A Chance of Meatballs* (2009)
- *Red Dawn* (2010)

International Weather Symbols: Rain

Light intermittent	•
Light continuous	••
Moderate intermittent	• • (vertically)
Moderate continuous	• • •
Heavy intermittent	• • •
Heavy continuous	• • • •

❋ ❋ ❋

The Original Cloud Spotters

Hamlet: Do you see yonder cloud that's almost in shape of a camel?

Polonius: By th' mass, and 'tis like a camel indeed.

Hamlet: Methinks it is like a weasel.

Polonius: It is back'd like a weasel.

Hamlet: Or a whale?

Polonius: Very like a whale.

William Shakespeare, *Hamlet*

The Man Who Named the Clouds

Until the start of the 19th century, there was no way to describe cloud forms other than the method used by Hamlet and Polonius. It was a British amateur meteorologist, Luke Howard, who established the well-known Latin classification system of cloud types still in use today. Howard was a manufacturing chemist by trade, but his passion was always the study of the weather. In his essay 'On the Modifications of Clouds and the principles of their production, suspension and destruction', published in the *Philosophical Magazine* in 1803, he divided clouds into genera and species, much as the animal and vegetable worlds had been categorised by the scientific innovative nomenclature of Carl Linnaeus in the previous century.

Having learned, through many canings at school, 'more Latin than he was able to forget', though not as much mathematics as he would have liked, he defined three basic groups: cumulus (a lump or heap), stratus (a layer) and cirrus (a wisp or curl of cloud). These 'genera' could be combined (e.g. cumulostratus, a lumpy layer cloud) and further modified according to secondary characteristics such as nimbus (rain-bearing), fractus (broken), and so on. Cumulonimbus is the heaped cloud associated with storms and precipitation; one of its subtypes is Cumulonimbus incus, the 'anvil cloud' with its characteristic flat top.

Howard lived in an era when scientists were allowed to retain some sense of poetry in their writing. 'The sky too belongs to the Landscape,' he wrote, 'the ocean of air in which we live and move, with its continents and islands of cloud, its tides and currents of constant and variable winds, is a component part of the great globe: and those regions in which the bolt of heaven is forged, and the fructifying rain condensed – where the cold hail concretes in the summer cloud – and from whence large masses of stone and metal have descended at times upon the earth – can never be to the zealous Naturalist a subject of tame and unfeeling contemplation.' He later painted watercolour sketches of 'his' clouds, and there is evidence that Constable, famous for his accurate artistic depictions of cloudscapes, was aware of Howard's work.

❋ ❋ ❋

When to Visit ... Barcelona

July
Av. daily sunshine: 10 hrs
Av. monthly rainfall: 1in (27mm)
Av. max. temperature: 28°C (82.4°F)

❋ ❋ ❋

A Joke For All Seasons

What game do tornadoes like to play?
Twister

❋ ❋ ❋

Record Weather: Snowiest

The greatest annual snowfall recorded was on Mount Rainier, Washington State, USA, where over 100ft (30.5m) of snow fell during the winter of 1972: to be precise, 1,244in (3,160cm) between February 1971 and February 1972. The record for the greatest amount of snow lying on the ground goes to Tamarack, California, for 451in (1,146cm) in March 1911. The greatest single snowfall was 169in (429cm) at Mount Shast Ski Bowl in California between 13 and 19 February 1959; 76in (193cm) fell in a single day at Silver Lake, Colorado, on 14–15 April 1921.

❈ ❈ ❈

Weather-related Baby Names (English)

- Aurora
- Autumn
- Celeste
- Cloud
- Dune
- Gail (Gale)
- Hailey

- Heavenly
- Kaia (Earth)
- Rain
- Rainbow
- Rayne
- Skye
- Star

- Stone
- Storm
- Summer
- Sunny/Sonny
- Sunshine
- Windy/Wendy
- Winter

❈ ❈ ❈

Fair Weather Fact

90% of people killed during hurricanes are drowned.

❋ ❋ ❋

Mother Nature's Tongue

English is a magpie language; it steals and coins words from anywhere it can, and ends up with a huge array of different ways of saying the same thing. And of course scientists can never use the everyday word for anything, they need a proper term of their own. Those who are addicted to stories about the number of words Eskimos have for snow will perhaps relish a quick survey of English adjectives connected with rain:

Pluvia (Latin): pluvial, pluvian, pluvious and pluviose. The last of these was one of the months in the French Revolutionary system.

Huetos (Greek): hyetal. This a technical meteorological term: a hyetologist might plot a hyetal chart using a rain gauge called a hyetograph, and join up the points of equal precipitation to make an isohyet.

❋ ❋ ❋

The Forecaster's Lament

And now among the fading embers
These in the main are my regrets
When I am right no one remembers
When I am wrong no one forgets.

Anon

❀ ❀ ❀

Whale Waste Saves the World?

Global warming is complicated stuff. It is easy enough to picture that car exhausts, jet engines, factory emissions and so on are not going to do any good to the polar icecaps, in sufficiently large amounts. However, it came as a surprise to many to learn just how major a role is played by methane emissions from cattle – cow flatulence, in other words. And, moving from the land to the oceans, whale faeces form another rather unexpected part of this complex formula.

As we no doubt all remember from school biology, photosynthesis is the process by which plants convert carbon dioxide into energy to live on. It's not just about how much carbon dioxide is produced, but also how much can be absorbed by this natural process. As emissions have increased, the means of disposing of them has decreased with the decimation of the world's enormous primeval forests. But trees are not the planet's only 'green lung'. Plankton, those tiny floating organisms that form the bottom rung of the marine food chain, come in three basic varieties: zooplankton (animals), bacterioplankton (bacteria) and phytoplankton (plants). Like terrestrial plants, they photosynthesise, absorbing hundreds of thousands of tons of carbon dioxide. They may not be as emotionally appealing to humans as rainforests or indeed whales, but they are crucial to the world's temperature. Their growth is controlled by the level of available nutrients including iron. Attempts have even been made to 'fertilise' the ocean by releasing iron in the hope of increasing carbon dioxide uptake. Whales play a more complicated role, however, for example, helping to move iron around the ocean by feeding at depth on squid, but excreting iron near the surface where the phytoplankton need it.

Mankind has yet to understand fully how phytoplankton can be harnessed to combat global warming, but meanwhile the whales have chalked up yet another good reason not to allow them to be hunted to extermination.

❈ ❈ ❈

Weather Playlist Part I: Oldies But Goodies

'Over the Rainbow' – Judy Garland
'Raining in My Heart' – Buddy Holly
'Summer Wind' – Frank Sinatra
    – T-Bone Walker
'Rainy Night in Georgia' – Brook Benton
'(Love is Like a) Heat Wave' – Martha and the Vandellas
'Stormy Weather' – Billie Holiday
'Here Comes the Flood' – Peter Gabriel
'Ain't No Sunshine' – Bill Withers

'Candle in the Wind' – Elton John
'I Wish it Would Rain Down' – Phil Collins
'Mr Blue Sky' – Electric Light Orchestra
'Purple Rain' – Prince
'Terminal Frost' – Pink Floyd
'The Tide is High' – Blondie
'You Are the Sunshine of My Life' – Stevie Wonder

❈ ❈ ❈

Fair Weather Fact

A falling raindrop travels as fast as 18mph (29km/h).

❈ ❈ ❈

Raining Cats and Dogs

The origins of this colourful English expression are, it seems safe to say, lost in the mists of time. It seems to go back at least as far as 1653, where we find the phrase 'It shall raine Dogs and Polecats' in a work by the English playwright Richard Brome. The polecats become cats in Jonathan Swift's *A Complete Collection of Polite and Ingenious Conversation* (1738): 'I know Sir John will go, though he was sure it would rain cats and dogs.'

As usual, there is no shortage of far-fetched explanations: it's all to do with the association between dogs and the Norse storm god Odin, or a corruption of a French word catadoupe, meaning a waterfall, which somehow mutated into 'cats and dogs'. Or perhaps you prefer this story: in the filthy streets of former centuries, cats and dogs would be drowned in the downpour and washed down the street, causing people to believe that they had fallen from the sky. Truly, the creative imagination knows few limits when it comes to inventing stories about word origins. As Jonathan Swift wrote in 'A Description of a City Shower':

Sweeping from butchers' stalls, dung, guts, and blood;
Drown'd puppies, stinking sprats, all drench'd in mud,
Dead cats, and turnip-tops, come tumbling down the flood.

Strange then that we do not speak of 'raining stinking sprats and turnip tops', though that would certainly have a certain ring to it. Alternatives to cats and dogs include chicken coops, stair-rods and hammer handles (none of these items especially likely to be seen choking the gutters after a storm), while, in America, pitchforks often feature: pitchforks and bullfrogs, pitchforks and grindstones, pitchforks and sawlogs, pitchforks and darning needles, pitchforks and barn shovels.

What do speakers of other languages say? In French, it rains nails (des clous), or cows (des vaches), or toads and cats (des crapauds et des chats). In German, pieces of string (Bindfäden) fall from the sky, which sounds safer than the Spanish equivalent of sticks with the points downwards (chuzos de punta). Perhaps Welsh wins the prize for the strangest forms of precipitation: either knives and forks (cyllyll a ffyrc) or old women and sticks (hen wragedd a ffyn). Did the bodies of female geriatrics come floating down the streets of Welsh towns, accompanied by not only theirwalking-sticks but also random items of cutlery?

Let There Be Light

12 And God said, 'This is the sign of the covenant I am making between me and you and every living creature with you, a covenant for all generations to come:

13 I have set my rainbow in the clouds, and it will be the sign of the covenant between me and the Earth.

14 Whenever I bring clouds over the earth and the rainbow appears in the clouds,

15 I will remember my covenant between me and you and all living creatures of every kind. Never again will the waters become a flood to destroy all life.

16 Whenever the rainbow appears in the clouds, I will see it and remember the everlasting covenant between God and all living creatures of every kind on the Earth.'

Genesis 9:12–16 (New International Version)

❈ ❈ ❈

Well Said...

Barometer, n. An ingenious instrument which indicates what kind of weather we are having.

❈ ❈ ❈

St Swithin's Day

Weather predictions are not limited to the increasingly glamorous, daily forecasts we see on television. Ancient traditions, as well as far-fetching folkore, also play their part in modern forecasting of the weather. Well, sort of.

The good people of Punxsutawney, Pennsylvania, for example, have their famous annual Groundhog Day on 2 February in which a groundhog's shadow (or lack thereof) can predict how much longer the winter season will last.

It may sound ridiculous, but in Britain we too have a similar method of weather 'prediction' – and it happens every 15 July, St Swithin's Day.

St Swithin was a 19th-century bishop whose bones were removed from his burial place at Winchester Cathedral. His disinterment was followed by 40 days of non-stop drizzle and bad weather. Now every 15 July, if it rains, the legend states that 40 days of downpours will ensue.

Met Office Records that date back to 1861 indicate that the UK's longest run of rain is 30 days – 10 days short of St Swithin's legacy. Until, however, in 2009, when the Isle of Skye experienced 31 days of continuous rain it seemed like the legend of St Swithin could finally become true. Of course, in the year 2006, the Isle of Skye saw 300 days of wet weather overall – so St Swithin's Day had become moot. As reported by the *Guardian* newspaper in 2009, St Swithin's Day in 1995 saw no rain and then experienced 38 days of dry weather.

✿ ✿ ✿

Winds of the World: Part I

- **Abroholos squall** – winter wind off the coast of eastern Brazil.
- **Aperwind, aberwind, alpach** – warm, thawing Alpine wind.
- **Bayamo** – severe tropical thundersquall on the south coast of Cuba.
- **Bentu de soli** – easterly wind on the coast of Sardinia.
- **Berg wind** – hot, dry mountain wind off the interior plateau of South Africa.
- **Bise, bize** – cold wind in central Switzerland and eastern France.
- **Bora** – northerly or north-easterly wind in the Adriatic, named after Boreas, the North Wind.
- **Brickfielder** – old Australian term for a wind that blew red dust over Sydney.
- **Brisa, briza** – north-easterly sea wind in South America.
- **Brisote** – north-easterly trade wind in Cuba.
- **Brubu** – squall in the East Indies.
- **Buran** – strong north-easterly wind in Russia, Siberia and central Asia; white buran when it carries snow in winter, black buran (karaburan) when it carries sand in summer.
- **Cape Doctor** – dry south-easterly wind on the South African coast, supposedly invigorating.
- **Cers, cierzo, narbonnais** – names for the mistral in parts of southern France and north-east Spain.
- **Chili (Tunisia), chichili (Algeria)** – hot dry wind similar to the sirocco.
- **Chinook** – warming mountain wind of the Pacific Northwest and western interior of North America.
- **Chocolatta north** – north-westerly gale in the West Indies.

- **Cordonazo** – southerly hurricane winds along the west coast of Mexico.
- **Diablo wind** – hot, dry north-easterly offshore wind typical of the San Francisco Bay area.
- **Dimmerfoehn, Dimmerfôhn** – strong southerly Alpine mountain wind.
- **Elephanta, elephant, elephanter** – southerly or south-easterly wind on the Malabar coast of India following the monsoon.
- **Etesian winds** – strong, dry northerly winds of the Aegean Sea.
- **Euroclydon** – classical name for the north-easterly wind of the Mediterranean.
- **Fremantle Doctor, Freo Doctor** – cool summer sea breeze on the coasts of Western Australia.
- **Ghibli, chibli, gebli, gibleh, gibli, kibli, qibl** – North African name for the hot dusty desert wind called the sirocco in the Mediterranean.
- **Gilavar** – warm southerly coastal wind in eastern Azerbaijan.
- **Gregale** – Maltese term for the north-easterly wind of the Mediterranean.
- **Halny wiatr** – mountain wind in southern Poland and Slovakia.
- **Harmattan** – hot, dry easterly or north-easterly winter wind in West Africa.
- **Helm wind** – strong cold north-easterly wind, which blows down the Cross Fell escarpment into the Eden valley in Cumbria; said to be the only named wind in the British Isles.

The Poet in Winter

The winter it is past, and the summer comes at last
And the small birds, they sing on ev'ry tree;
Now ev'ry thing is glad, while I am very sad,
Since my true love is parted from me.

Robert Burns, 'The Winter it is Past'

❋ ❋ ❋

When to Visit ... New Orleans

April
Av. daily sunshine: 8 hrs
Av. monthly rainfall: 4½ in (114mm)
Av. max. temperature: 25°C (77°F)

❈ ❈ ❈

International Weather Symbols: Snow

Light intermittent	✳
Light continuous	✳ ✳
Moderate intermittent	✳ ✳
Moderate continuous	✳ ✳ ✳
Heavy intermittent	✳ ✳ ✳
Heavy continuous	✳ ✳ ✳
Mixed rain and snow	⍗
Drifting snow	⍗

Seven Things You Never Wanted to Know About Global Warming

1. Average temperatures are 0.8°C (1.4°F) higher around the world since 1880.

2. The decades 1980 and 1990 were the hottest in 400 years and possibly the warmest for several millennia.

3. Arctic ice is rapidly disappearing. By 2040 the area may see its first ice-free summer.

4. Sea levels could rise between 7 and 23in (18–59cm) by 2100. Rises of just 4in (10cm) could mean many low-lying islands and large parts of South-East Asia could become seriously flooded.

5. Over one hundred million people live within 3ft (1m) of mean sea level, and a high percentage of the world's population lives local to coastal cities.

6. More than one million species face extinction from disappearing habitat, changing ecosystems and acidifying oceans.

7. The ocean conveyor belt, the earth's circulation system, could be permanently altered, causing a mini-ice age in Western Europe.

❉ ❉ ❉

Seasonal Recipes
Spring Lamb Casserole

Preparation Time 30 minutes · Cooking Time about 1 ¾ hours · Serves 12 · Per Serving 307 calories, 15g fat (of which 5g saturates), 18g carbohydrate, 0.5g salt · Dairy Free

3 tbsp olive oil
2½lb (1.1kg) boneless shoulder of spring lamb, chopped into 1½in (4cm) cubes – remove excess fat and gristle
18fl oz (500ml) hot vegetable stock
1 tsp each smoked paprika, ground cinnamon and coriander
2 rosemary sprigs
2 large onions, each cut into 12–14 wedges
11oz (300g) Chantenay carrots, trimmed
4oz (125g) ready-to-eat dried apricots, roughly chopped
½ pint (300ml) dry white wine
2 × 400g cans chickpeas, drained and rinsed
Salt and ground black pepper
Mixed green vegetables to serve

1   Heat half the olive oil in a large flameproof casserole and brown the lamb pieces in batches. Set aside in a bowl.

2   Pour a little of the hot stock into the pan. Scrape the bottom with a wooden spoon to release any sticky goodness, then pour it over the reserved lamb. Heat the remaining oil in the pan and stir in the spices, rosemary, onions, carrots and apricots. Cook for one minute.

3 Stir in the wine, the remaining stock and half the
chickpeas, then return the lamb to the pan. Cover and
bring to the boil. Reduce the heat and simmer for 1½
hours, stirring occasionally, until the lamb is tender.

4 Meanwhile, mash the remaining chickpeas. Stir into the
finished casserole and check the seasoning. Remove the
rosemary stalks and serve with vegetables.

❊ ❊ ❊

Weather-related Street Names: London

• Air Street (W1) • Half Moon Street (W1)
• Ray Street (EC1) • Sunbeam Road (NW10) • Snow Hill
(EC1) • Spring Gardens (SW1) • Sunray Avenue (SE24)
• Water Lane (EC3) • Apollo Place (E11) • Weatherley
Close (E3) • Snowdrop Close (SE20) • Tideway Close
(TW10) • Windy Ridge Close (SW19) • Summerwood Road
(TW7) • Rainville Road (W6)• Windrush Close (W4)
• Summers Row (N12) • Sunny Avenue (SE24)
• Sunset Road (SE5)

❊ ❊ ❊

Cloud Names (scientific)

Clouds are scientifically categorised according to shape and height in a system devised by British amateur meteorologist Luke Howard in 1803. Their internationally recognised Latin names resemble the scientific names of living organisms, with a genus and species, and 'subspecies' are also possible. The World Meteorological Organization allows 10 'genera' of cloud: Cirrus (Ci), Cirrocumulus (Cc), Cirrostratus (Cs), Altocumulus (Ac), Altostratus (As), Nimbostratus (Ns), Cumulus (Cu), Stratocumulus (Sc), Stratus (St) and Cumulonimbus (Cb).

Much of the time a broad term like cumulus, cirrus, cumulonimbus or altostratus will be sufficient, but to that can be added 'species' names like fractus (broken, ragged), undulatus (wavy) or lenticularis (lens-shaped). Cumulonimbus incus means a thundercloud with the distinctive anvil shape, while Cumulonimbus pileus refers to one with an extra 'cap' or hood of cloud above it. These names have abbreviated forms, such as Cu fra for Cumulus fractus.

Tullius Stratocumulus is not a cloud, but the commander of a Roman garrison in *Asterix in Britain*.

Here are some cloud species and their abbreviations:

Calvus	cal	bald, smooth
Capillatus	cap	frayed, fibrous
Castellanus	cas	turret-like
Congestus	con	heaped
Fibratus	fib	thin, fibrous
Floccus	flo	tufted
Fractus	fra	broken, ragged
Humilis	hum	low, flattened

Lenticularis	len	lens-shaped
Mediocris	med	medium-sized
Nebulosus	neb	indistinct
Spissatus	spi	thick
Uncinus	unc	hooked (cirrus)

There are also amorphous clouds, ones without any apparent structure at all.

❈ ❈ ❈

When to Visit ... Cape Town

January
Av. daily sunshine: 11 hrs
Av. monthly rainfall: ½in (12mm)
Av. max. temperature: 26°C (78.8°F)

❈ ❈ ❈

Touched by the Hand of God?

Around 70% of people hit by lightning do survive. Lightning strikes can damage memory, vision, hearing and speech, as well as causing depression and apparently impotence.

So far so unsurprising, perhaps, but much odder effects have been reported too. While lightning is unlikely to be available on the NHS any time soon, in rare cases positive effects have been claimed. It is said to have restored the eyesight of a man who had lost it in a car crash 10 years before; he even claimed hair started to grow again on his bald head. The case of an American surgeon called Tony Cicori, documented by Oliver Sachs, is certainly intriguing. He was struck at a public telephone shortly after putting the phone down. Afterwards, he had memory problems for a while but they soon went away and nothing abnormal showed up on an MRI scan and an EEG. Then, despite never having been particularly musical, he developed a kind of obsession with the piano. He taught himself to play to a high standard, started composing and became something of a celebrity. Musical talent is often seen as a gift from the heavens, but high-voltage aerial delivery is not normally part of the picture.

❉ ❉ ❉

A Joke For All Seasons

'Gosh, it's raining cats and dogs,' said Fred looking out of the kitchen window.

'I know,' said his mother, 'I've just stepped in a poodle!'

Fair Weather Fact

The fastest winds on Earth occur inside a tornado
funnel where speeds as high as 300mph (483km/h)
have been recorded.

❄ ❄ ❄

Snow in the Deep South

In the southern United States in 2004, New Orleans saw its
first white Christmas in half a century and Houston its first
ever, and the first snow in living memory fell in such unlikely
places as Brownsville, Texas, and its twin city in Mexico,
Matamoros. Of course, December snow is rare in the
Southern Hemisphere, but Christmas morning 2005 saw the
Snowy Mountains of New South Wales and Victoria in
Australia under nearly 12in (30.5cm) of snow – in the bleak
midsummer.

❄ ❄ ❄

Well Said...

One need only think of the weather, in which case the
prediction even for a few days ahead is impossible.

Albert Einstein, physicist

Places Named With the Weather in Mind

Costa del Sol (Spain) – the sunny coast

Nevada (USA) – Spanish for 'snowfall'

Windscale (Cumbria) – Norse for 'a windy place with huts'

Dryburgh (Scottish Borders) – a dry fortress, perhaps meaning one unreachable by floods

Iceland – biggest glaciers in Europe; previously known as Snæland (Snowland)

Greenland – the southern part, free of glaciers, is green in the summer

Windward/Leeward Isles – on the side facing/away from the wind, with respect to ships arriving in the West Indies, where the prevailing trade winds blow east to west

Snowshill – a snowy hill in Gloucestershire

❊　❊　❊

An Inconvenient Truth

Unlike the big budget Hollywood fanfare of movies such as the *The Day After Tomorrow* (2006), and *2012* (2009), which delve into the weather-obsessed end-of-the-world scenario with gusto, former US Vice President Al Gore's heroic, low-key effort, *An Inconvenient Truth* (2006), received much commercial and critical success – and helped to earn Gore the Nobel Peace Prize in the process. It's a movie very much about the end of the world as we know it, but, instead of unrealistic CGI and clichéd plot, it is Gore standing alone in front of an overhead projector and a scissor lift telling a shocked audience just how bad global warming really is going to get. It's captivating viewing full of horrifying statistics, retreating icecaps and graphs with lines that keep going up.

If you don't recycle yet, watch this film, and you will.

❈ ❈ ❈

Medical Effects of Weather

The weather has a huge range of effects on health and wellbeing.Perhaps the most obvious consideration is temperature. Human beings, even more so than most animals, need to maintain a very steady core body temperature – a state of 'homeothermy' – of 36.5–37.5°C (98–100°F), and even quite slight variations can be serious. If the temperature drops below 35°C (95°F), the result is hypothermia – what used to be called exposure – and this can kill with surprising speed. The victim may become confused and aggressive, look cold but may actually feel too hot, as their brains lose the ability to gauge body temperature accurately: mountaineers suffering from hypothermia often throw away vital equipment and actually remove warm clothing ('paradoxical undressing').

However, extreme cooling can sometimes save a life. People who are rescued unconscious after falling into freezing water are sometimes revived up to an hour later, the cold having shut down their metabolic systems to such an extent that they were able to survive with less oxygen.

Since cold restricts the circulation in the extremities, it can cause tissue damage, such as chilblains (skin ulcers caused by cold), and in more severe cases frostnip (skin cooling without permanent damage) or frostbite (where cells are destroyed and whole fingers or toes may die). The cold also reduces our resistance to infection, and also infectious diseases may spread more rapidly when people tend to spend more time crowded together indoors.

Heat is just as dangerous as cold. The name for medical overheating is hyperthermia, which is defined as a body temperature exceeding 37.5(100°F). Heavy sweating dehydrates the body and deprives it of salt, causing cramps. Other symptoms include heat exhaustion (heavy sweating, rapid breathing, fast, weak pulse), heat rash, syncope (fainting), tetany (spasms) and oedema (swelling). The result of body temperatures of over 40.6°C (105.1°F) is heat stroke, which causes mental confusion and can be fatal.

In hot weather, bacteria thrive, contributing to the spread of disease through spoiled food. Wet conditions favour insect-borne diseases, notably malaria, spread by mosquitoes whose life cycle requires warm and wet conditions. Warm, dry weather in spring and summer allows pollen to circulate freely, causing misery to hay-fever sufferers.

Excessive humidity can be very dangerous. The body's natural cooling mechanism is evaporation through sweating, which becomes less effective the more moist the air is. If the humidity is near 100%, in other words the air cannot hold any more moisture, then sweat cannot evaporate from the skin; if the air temperature approaches the maximum temperature the body can tolerate, the conditions are life-threatening, especially for the old and infirm. In the Mediterranean, the combination of summer heat and high humidity quite often kills hundreds of people. The heatwave of July 1987 in Athens was said to have been the cause of around a thousand deaths.

Prolonged exposure to wet conditions can cause skin complaints including so-called 'trench foot', first recorded in Napoleon's troops during the retreat from Russia in 1812, and more famously during the First World War.

Dry weather can cause dermatitis, and changes in humidity and pressure are often claimed to affect not only arthritis but also phantom pains in amputees, perhaps because scar tissue expands and contracts at a different rate to the surrounding skin.

The weather can affect the human mind in all sorts of ways. Heatwaves are often associated with violence, such as murder and domestic incidents. A 75% hike was recorded in the homicide rate in New York in the heatwave of 1988. The seasonal thawing of ice in arctic regions can apparently cause a kind of collective hysteria. Certain winds are seriously believed to have mental effects so significant that, for example, the Italian sirocco and the foehn wind of the Alps have actually been considered as mitigating circumstances in court cases.

❈ ❈ ❈

A Joke For All Seasons

There's a technical term for a sunny, warm day that follows two rainy days – it's called Monday.

❈ ❈ ❈

William on Weather: Part I

… the spring, the summer,
The chilling autumn, angry winter, change
Their wonted liveries; and the mazed world
By their increase, now knows not which is which.
A Midsummer Night's Dream

Blow, blow, thou winter wind,
Thou art not so unkind
As man's ingratitude
As You Like It

Is not their climate foggy, raw and dull,
On whom, as in despite, the sun looks pale,
Killing their fruit with frowns?
Henry V

When that I was and a little tiny boy,
With hey, ho, the wind and the rain,
A foolish thing was but a toy,
For the rain it raineth every day.
Twelfth Night

❈ ❈ ❈

Weathering Heights

The planet's atmosphere is divided into levels, each with their own distinct composition and personality:

- **Troposphere:** 11 miles (17.7km) above the ground. This is where the weather happens. Most clouds found here. Temperature decreases with altitude.

- **Stratosphere:** 11–31 miles (17.7–50km) above the ground. Slight temperature increase. Ozone layer located here.

- **Mesosphere:** 31–50 miles (50–80.5km) above the ground. Temperatures drop rapidly with increasing height. The area between the mesosphere and outer space is known as the thermosphere; here, temperatures increase with altitude.

- **Ionosphere:** 50–400 miles (80.5–644km) above the ground. Made up of ionized gases that reflect radio waves and allow worldwide radio communication.

- **Exosphere:** 400+ miles (644+ km) above the ground. Outer limits of the earth's atmosphere.

❈ ❈ ❈

The Rain Man

George James Symons, the man who was nicknamed the 'rain man', will have his well-weathered memorial rededicated by the Royal Meteorological Society at Kensal Green cemetery in London in 2010.

In 1860, Symons founded the British Rainfall Organisation and his revolutionary work provided evidence, statistics and figures to support which downpours were the worst, longest or rarest – effectively coining the well-known weather phrase, 'since records began'.

And if you thought weathermen never had a sense of humour, think again. Symons's now-damaged burial grave stone was originally cut from the Honister quarry in Seathwaite, a region that is regularly recorded as having the UK's highest annual rainfall since, you guessed it, records began.

❈ ❈ ❈

Lore and Order

Red sky at night, shepherd's delight,
Red sky in morning, shepherd's warning.

❈ ❈ ❈

SPRING

International Weather Symbols: Storms

Thunderstorm	
Heavy thunderstorm	
Tropical storm	
Hurricane	
Squall	
Sandstorm	
Polar Aurora	
Dust devils	
Lightning	
Calm	

Weather by The Masters
(Well, some of them)

Upper portion of The Crucifixion
Jan van Eyck (c.1435)

View of Toledo
El Greco (1597)

A Study of Clouds
John Constable (1822)

The Storm (Shipwreck)
JMW Turner (1823)

Hut in Snow
Caspar David Friedrich (1826)

A Rainy Season in the Tropics
Frederic E. Church (1866)

Regatta at Sainte-Adresse
Claude Monet (1867)

Grey Weather
Claude Monet (1892)

Snow Scene at Eragny
Camille Pissarro (1894)

Hurricane — Bahamas
Winslow Homer (1899)

The Poet in Summer

A something in a summer's Day
As slow her flambeaux burn away
Which solemnizes me.

A something in a summer's noon
A depth – an Azure – a perfume
Transcending ecstasy.

And still within a summer's night
A something so transporting bright
I clap my hands to see –

Emily Dickinson, '122'

Weather Cocktails: Part II

Highland Moon Scotch, drambuie, slice of lemon and a maraschino cherry.

East Wind Vodka, dry vermouth, sweet red vermouth, slice of orange, slice of lemon.

Galway Sunrise Drambuie, orange juice, vodka, triple sec, Frothee.

Triple Sun Vodka, banana-flavoured liquer, sweet white vermouth, dry vermouth, 2 dashes grenadine, 1 maraschino cherry.

Blue Day Vodka, blue caracao, 1 dash orange bitters, half-slice orange.

Nordic Summer Orange juice, vodka, passion-fruit syrup, lime juice, dash of grenadine, slice of lime, 1 maraschino cherry.

Hoarfrost Gin, white curacao, light rum, grenadine, lemon juice.

After the Storm Gin, light cream, scotch, white crème de cacao, 1 maraschino cherry.

Northern Light Gin, cassis, triple sec, lemon juice, 1 dash Frothee, 1 maraschino cherry.

Record Weather: Wettest

The highest annual rainfall is in Mawsynram in India, where some 467in (11,862mm) of rain have been recorded. The most rain in one day was on the island of La Rèunion in the Indian Ocean on 16 March 1952: 70in (1,778mm). On Guadeloupe on 26 November 1970, 1½in (38mm) fell in a single minute.

Cloud Families

Clouds are grouped into families by altitude. The WMO classification uses the French term 'étage': high étage (2–5 miles/3–8km); middle étage (1¼–21/2 miles/2–4km); and low étage (surface to 1¼ miles/2km).

Family	Altitude (depending on region)	Species	Comments
A (high)	10,000–60,000ft (3,048–18,288m)	Cirrus (Ci) Cirrocumulus (Cc), Cirrostratus (Cs)	Primarily composed of ice crystals
B (middle)	6,500–25,000ft (1,981–7,620m)	Altocumulus (Ac), Altostratus (As), Nimbostratus (Ns)	Can be water droplets or ice
C (low)	Below 6,500ft (1,981m)	Cumulus (Cu), Stratocumulus (Sc), Stratus (St), Nimbostratus (Ns)	Mostly water droplets
D (vertical)	Many heights	Cumulus (Cu), Cumulonimbus (Cb)	Can grow to heights up to about 40,000ft (12,192m)

Fair Weather Fact

Snowflakes falling at 2–4mph (3.2–6.4km/h) can take about one hour to reach the ground.

Top 10 Things to Take to a British Music Festival*

1. Thermal socks
2. Thermal underpants
3. Wellington boots
4. Bin liners (for the muddy Wellington boots)
5. Allergy tablets
6. Poncho
7. Wet wipes
8. Sun cream
9. Sunglasses
10. Toilet roll

*In case of unexpected weather – to be expected

It Makes Sense...

The weather vane will not work without wind.
(Maltese proverb)

When to Visit ... Paris

June
Av. daily sunshine: 8 hrs
Av. monthly rainfall: 2in (54mm)
Av. max. temperature: 23°C (73.4°F)

Dog Days

Dog Days is the name given to the very hot summer weather
that persists for 4–6 weeks between mid-July and early
September in the United States. In western Europe, this
period may exist from the first week in July to mid-August
and is often the period of the greatest frequency of thunder.
Named after Sirius, the Dog Star, which lies in conjunction
with the sun during this period, it was once believed to
intensify the sun's heat during the summer months.

The Great Hinckley Fire

In September 1894, a firestorm of positively Biblical proportions descended on a thriving town in the American Midwest, destroying it so completely that it has never recovered. Its prosperity, and its downfall, was the logging industry. The official death-toll was 418, but many were never found; bodies were still being found five years later, and the true number of fatalities may be nearer 600 or even 800.

Hinckley, about 70 miles (113km) north of Minneapolis, was the hub of a logging operation covering a large area in the aptly named Pine County, Minnesota. The smaller settlements of Mission Creek and Brook Park lay nearby. It had been a dry summer, with no rain for two months. The land was like the proverbial tinder-box, made even more dangerous by the way timber was harvested: loggers would either leave their 'slash', the unwanted twigs and branches, lying on the forest floor, providing rich fuel for fire, or dispose of it by burning it. Perhaps it was such fires that started a conflagration that took only four hours to destroy an area of over 400 square miles (1,036km²).

Even so, it would not have been so disastrous without a third factor: the weather. A temperature inversion, a layer of cold air above warmer air, caused powerful downward winds when the heat burst through into the upper layer, and literally fanned the flames. This is known as a firestorm, a sort of tornado of fire racing across the ground at enormous speed, with temperatures reaching 500°C (1,000°F) and heating the air ahead so intensely that trees simply burst into flame. An even worse firestorm, the Cloquet Fire, struck Minnesota in 1918. Even today mankind is largely powerless against this terrifying phenomenon; in August 1988, over one third of Yellowstone National Park was turned to ashes by dozens of fires, leaving the terrain so damaged that dead trees were still a danger 20 years later.

In an era before fire-fighting planes, rescue helicopters and so on, the loss of life was truly horrifying. One James Root, a train driver, managed to evacuate nearly 300 people on a train to a place called Skunk Lake, about 5 miles (8km) from Hinckley, where the passengers were able to escape the fire; but mostly people perished where they stood, and perhaps as many disappeared without trace as were accounted for. One of the presumed victims was a Union soldier, a certain Thomas P. 'Boston' Corbett. He is famous as the assassin of John Wilkes Booth, none other than the man who shot President Abraham Lincoln.

The Poet in Summer

Great is the sun, and wide he goes
Through empty heaven with repose;
And in the blue and glowing days
More thick than rain he showers his rays.

Robert Louis Stevenson, 'Summer Sun'

The Shipping Forecast

'And now the shipping forecast, issued by the Met Office on behalf of the Maritime and Coastguard Agency at double-oh one five today...'

Who would have thought the bare bones of weather warnings for coastal shipping, broadcast at the unsocial extreme ends of the day's radio schedules, could have become such a national icon? The forecasts are easy to decode if you know what each phrase refers to. First comes the wind direction and speed, then the sea state, then the weather, and finally visibility. 'Southerly, veering westerly 5 or 6, occasionally variable 7 later... Moderate or rough... Occasional drizzle... Good.' This crisp telegraphic format has often been claimed to have a sort of austere poetry.

They also offer comic possibilities, tickling the imagination of, for example, the performance poet Les Barker: 'Forties, Fifties, Sixties, Tyne, Dogger, German Bight, French kiss and Swiss roll ... Hebrides, Bailey, Fair Isle, Cardigan, Pullover and South-east Iceland: wind south east, rain at times, slightly disappointing'.

The list in full, however, goes a little something like this:

Bailey – Biscay – Cromarty – Dogger – Dover – Faeroes – Fair Isle – Fastnet – Fisher – FitzRoy (formerly Finisterre) – Forth Forties – German Bight – Hebrides – Humber – Irish Sea – Lundy – Malin – North Utsire – Plymouth – Portland – Rockall Shannon – Sole – South Utsire – Southeast Iceland – Thames Trafalgar – Tyne – Viking – Wight

Top 10 British Weather Disasters: Part 1

1. **The Great Storm of 1703**: On 26 November 1973, a great storm caused widespread damage across England and Wales. Winds were estimated to have exceeded 120mph (193km/h) and houses, trees and even churches were demolished. Estimates of the number of people killed on land and at sea ranges from 8,000 to 15,000.

2. **The Great Smog of 1952**: Ever since the Industrial Revolution, smog became a frequent part of life in towns and cities in the UK. However, for four long days in December 1952, a smoke-laden fog covered the whole of London. It was so thick and polluted that it left thousands dead, reduced visibility to just a few feet and brought transport to a standstill.

3. **East Coast Floods 1953**: Exceptional weather conditions combined with high spring tides produced one of the worst floods on the East coast. The storm surge killed 307 people and flooded 147,000 acres (100,000ha). The damage cost the equivalent of £5 billion in today's money.

4. **The Great Derby Day Disaster 1911**: Severe thunderstorms hit the south-east of England on 31 May 1911. Two and a half inches (62mm) of rain fell on Epsom Downs in 50 minutes (3½in/92mm by the time the storm ended). Around 5.30pm there were 159 lightning flashes in just 15 minutes; many of the spectators were struck and three died.

5. **The Harsh Winter of 1947:** In the aftermath of the
   Second World War, the UK experienced an exceptionally
   cold winter. Two short spells of cold weather (in December
   1946 and early January 1947) were followed by a cold snap
   that lasted from 21 January to 16 March. The coldest
   temperature recorded was -21°C (-5.8°F) at Woburn in
   Buckinghamshire. During this period snow fell
   somewhere in the country for 55 consecutive days.

Under the Weather: Part I
(Weather clichés for all seasons)

- It's darkest just before the dawn
- It's raining cats and dogs
- It will be a cold day in hell
- For everything there is a season
- After the rain comes a rainbow
- Every cloud has a silver lining
- Full of hot air

Quaint Weather Terms

Proof, were it needed, that when it comes to language, the British are a weird bunch ...

All-hallow Summer   A period of unexpected, unseasonable warmth.

Blunk   A sudden increase in wind speed, or squall.

Cat's Nose   A cool, north-westerly wind.

Dimpsey   Very dull, wet weather conditions with low cloud and fine drizzle. Commonly used in Cornwall and Devon.

Flanders Storm   Heavy fall of snow coming in from a southern wind.

Gowsty / Gusty   Most commonly used in Northumberland.

Hurly-burly   A massive thunderstorm.

Kelsher   A heavy rainfall.

Moor-gallop   An unexpected increase in wind speed across the moors.

Northern Nanny   A cold hail and wind storm in Northern England.

Mizzle   Very fine, but dense rain. A combination of mist and drizzle

Robin Hood's Wind   A local Yorkshire term for a cold north-easterly wind along the east coast.

Scorcher   An extremely hot day in the UK.

Sailing By

It's strange how random pieces of trivia can evolve into the icons of national consciousness. For many a British expat, an irritating little ditty called 'Sailing By' has acquired the feeling of comfort and security a child might obtain from a favourite blanket. For many years, it has introduced the late-night shipping forecast broadcast on Radio 4 just before it battens down the hatches for the night. This is because of the broadcast frequencies used by BBC network radio, =; Radio 4 occupies the one best suited to long-distance reception (until 1978 for Radio 2): 200 kHz, or 1500 metres if you prefer.

Radio 4 Long Wave comes to the lonely mariner and the confirmed Luddite principally from Droitwich, where a T-aerial suspended between two 700ft- (213m-) high guyed steel lattice masts 590ft (180m) apart may be seen gleaming in the moonlight. No less than half a megawatt of 'Sailing By' thunders out from them every night shortly after midnight. With its syrupy strings and chugging guitars, it may be an annoying little earworm of a melody, but it's somehow part of the DNA of the lifelong Radio 4 listener. Some find it positively restful. Jarvis Cocker, once famous as the lead singer of Pulp, found it such a useful 'aid to restful sleep' that he chose it as one of his Desert Island Discs. In 1997 it finally became available commercially on an EMI Classics CD set grandly entitled *The Great British Experience*: Fifty Original Light Music Classics (EMI CDGB50, track 11 on CD2, if you're interested).

The proportion of the (non-maritime) Radio 4 audience that still listens on Long Wave is very small, despite a passionate campaign to save it some years ago, but it has a kind of special status in the hearts of the Radio 4 tribe.

Weather-related Street Names: Edinburgh

**Castle Wynd North • Castle Wynd South •
Fairmile Avenue • Hailes Crescent • Seaview Terrace
• Sunnybank • Sunnyside• Watergate**

Fair Weather Fact

In New York in 1988, the temperature stayed above 32°C
(89.6°C) for 32 days and the murder rate soared by 75%.

Record Weather: Largest Hailstone

On 14 April 1986, a hailstone weighing just under 2¼lb (1kg)
fell in the Gopalanj district of Bangladesh. Ninety-two people
were killed.

Bob Dylan's Weather Top Ten
(Rated in order of severity)

'Hurricane' (1975)
'Shelter From the Storm' (1975)
'Down in the Flood' (1961)
'High Water' (2001)
'A Hard Rain's A-gonna Fall' (1962)
'Four Strong Winds' (1967)
'Blowin' In The Wind' (1963)
'Idiot Wind' (1975)
'Buckets of Rain' (1975)
'Rainy Day Women No. 12 & 35' (1966)

When to Visit ... New York

June
Av. daily sunshine: 10 hrs
Av. monthly rainfall: 3¼in (86mm)
Av. max. temperature: 26°C (78.8°F)

Lightning Flowers

Nature loves a branching structure: branches, roots, leaf veins, blood vessels – it's almost a kind of trademark of creation, on our planet at least. These structures have the same strange beauty as fractals, Fibonacci numbers or the ratio known as the Golden Mean.

Lightning forks and branches too, and not just as it travels through the air where we can see it, but through any insulating material through which it forges its way, constantly spreading, questing and sending out tentacles (known as leaders) that succeed or fail to find their way to earth more directly than their fellows. These are known as Lichtenberg figures (Lichtenberg-Figuren) after the 18th-century German physicist Georg Christoph Lichtenberg who discovered them, and they are indeed thought to be a type of fractal, considered to extend down to molecular level. You can produce this effect deliberately, as Lichtenberg did, by discharging a high-voltage charge through a sharp point on to an insulating surface, leaving a pattern of charge on the surface, which can then be dusted with (say) sulphur powder to reveal these fascinating images. Nowadays, you can buy the results in a Perspex block as an ornament.

The effect is also known, more poetically, as 'lightning flowers'. However, one example where they occur in less charming circumstances is on the bodies of victims of lightning strikes. The medical term is arborescent erythema, or sometimes keraunographic markings. These sinister red traceries, caused by (it is believed) ruptured capillaries, branch and snake over the skin rather like ferns; they may fade after hours or days, and provide a classic diagnostic tool for the pathologist.

A Christmas Number One

The song 'White Christmas' by Irving Berlin was first publicly performed on NBC radio on Christmas Day 1941 by Bing Crosby, who sang it in the 1942 musical *Holiday Inn*; it won an Oscar for Best Original Song and single sold 50 million copies. And it topped the charts three times in the 1940s, once for 11 weeks, which is much better than the recent wave – in the UK at least – of dire *X Factor* Christmas singles.

Whether the Weather...

Whether the weather be fine,
Whether the weather be not,
Whether the weather be cold,
Whether the weather be hot,
We'll weather the weather,
Whatever the weather,
Whether we like it or not.

Anon

Cloud Symbols: High Clouds

High clouds are found at 10,000–60,000ft (3,048–18,288m). These symbols are used by meteorologists for recording the types, combinations and development of clouds.

1. Cirrus

2. Dense cirrus

3. Dense cirrus derived
   from cumulonimbus

4. Hook-shaped cirrus
   spreading and thickening

5. Cirrus or cirrostratus
   spreading and thickening
   not more than 45° above horizon

6. As above but bulk of cloud
   more than 45° above horizon

7. Cirrostratus covering entire sky.

8. Cirrostratus not increasing,
   not covering entire sky

9. Cirrocumulus or mainly cirrocumulus
   with other cirriform clouds

The Great Storm: Part I

'Earlier on today, apparently, a woman rang the BBC and said she heard there was a hurricane on the way. Well, if you're watching, don't worry, there isn't!'

Michael Fish, BBC weatherman, on the eve of 'The Great Storm of 1987', which killed 19 people and was the worst storm to hit south-east England since 1703.

When to Visit ... Rio de Janeiro

February
Av. daily sunshine: 7 hrs
Av. monthly rainfall: 5in (122mm)
Av. max. temperature: 29°C (84.2°F)

Fair Weather Fact

One cubic mile (4km³) of ordinary fog contains less than a gallon of water.

Seasonal Recipes
Summer Fruit Brûlée

Preparation Time 15 minutes, plus macerating and standing
Cooking Time 3–4 minutes · Serves 4 · Per Serving 270
calories, 21g fat, 16g carbohydrate

1 ripe nectarine, halved, stoned and thinly sliced
12oz (350g) mixed summer berries, such as strawberries,
blackberries, raspberries and redcurrants
2 tbsp ruby port
¼ pint (150ml) double cream
4oz (125g) Greek-style yogurt
A few drops of vanilla extract
1oz (25g) Demerara sugar

1 Put the nectarine and summer berries into a bowl, add the
   port and stir to mix. Leave to macerate for 1–2 hours if
   possible. Transfer to a 1½ pint (900ml) gratin dish.

2 Whip the cream in a bowl until it holds its shape, then fold
   in the yogurt together with the vanilla extract. Spread the
   cream mixture evenly over the fruit, to cover completely.

3 Scatter the Demerara sugar over the cream and grill under
   a high heat as close to the heat source as possible for 3–4
   minutes until the sugar is golden brown and caramelised.
   (Alternatively, you can wave a cook's blowtorch over the
   surface to caramelise the sugar.) Leave to stand for five
   minutes, then serve.

Record Weather: Windiest

The windiest place on the planet is Commonwealth Bay on the George V Coast of Antarctica, where winds of 200mph (322km/h) have been recorded. The highest wind speed ever recorded was 230mph (370km/h) at Mount Washington in New Hampshire, USA, on 20 March 1986. The highest tornado wind speed was at Wichita Falls, Texas, 2 April 1958: an incredible 280mph (451km/h).

Super Snow People

The record for the world's tallest snowman used to belong to 'Angus, King of the Mountain', created by the residents of the American town of Bethel, Maine, United States, in February 1999. He was named after Angus S. King, Jr, the 72nd governor of the state (1995–2003). At 113ft 7in tall (34.62m), he took two weeks to build and apparently had whole trees for arms.

However, in 2008 Angus was beaten – and by a snow woman. This frosty Amazon measured just over 122ft (37.2m), weighed nearly 6 tons and boasted truck tyres for buttons and skis for eyelashes (16 skis in fact). How do we know she was a woman? Why, because her name was Olympia Snowe, after a Maine senator of the same irresistibly appropriate name.

Top 10 British Beaches (in Summer)

1. Bournemouth, Dorset
2. West Wittering, West Sussex
3. Croyde Bay, North Devon
4. Holy Island, Northumberland
5. Holkham, Norfolk
6. Great Bay, St Martin's, Isles of Scilly
7. Blackpool, Lancashire
8. Abereiddi Blue Lagoon, Pembrokeshire
9. Sinclair's Bay, Caithness
10. Porthcurno, Cornwall

Here Comes The Sun

Real weather-related pub names in Britain

The Sun Burnt Arms
The Iso Bar
The Sun Inn
The Half Moon
Moon Under the Water
John Snow
Rising Sun
The Bell Wether

The Rainbow Inn
The Mad Dog in the Fog
Foggy's
The Weather Vane
The Thomas Frost
The Four Seasons
The Fulflood Arms
Aire of the Dog

The Poet in Summer

Shall I compare thee to a summer's day?
Thou art more lovely and more temperate;
Rough winds do shake the darling buds of May,
And summer's lease hath all too short a date;
Sometime too hot the eye of heaven shines,
And often is his gold complexion dimm'd;
And every fair from fair sometime declines,
By chance or nature's changing course untrimm'd;
But thy eternal summer shall not fade,
Nor lose possession of that fair thou ow'st;
Nor shall Death brag thou wander'st in his shade,
When in eternal lines to time thou grow'st:
So long as men can breathe or eyes can see,
So long lives this, and this gives life to thee.

William Shakespeare, 'Sonnet 18'

The Enhanced Fujita (EF) Scale

This scale, based on one invented by Ted Fujita in 1971, has been used since 2007 to measure the strength of tornadoes in the United States, from 0 to 5. It was first applied to tornadoes in eastern Florida measuring EF3. The first EF5 tornado was at Greensburg, Kansas, on 4 May 2007.

Category	Wind speed (mph, km/h)	Damage
0	65–85, 105–137	None or minor: branches broken; shallow-rooted trees pushed over; damage to roofs and gutters.
1	86–110, 138–177	Moderate: roofs badly damaged; mobile homes overturned; glass broken; doors ripped off.
2	111–135, 179–217	Considerable: large trees uprooted or broken; roofs torn off; mobile homes destroyed; cars lifted.
3	136–165, 219–266	Severe: trees de-barked; trains overturned; large, strong buildings damaged; weak structures blown away.
4	166–200, 267–322	Extreme: houses levelled; cars thrown about.
5	200+, 322+	Total: strong houses blown away; steel-reinforced concrete buildings and high-rise buildings badly damaged.

Flight of Fancy

Seagull, seagull, sit on the sand.
It's never good weather when you're on land.

Potholes

Winter is hard on roads. No surface has yet been devised that can withstand anything the weather throws at it. The mixture of rock chippings and bitumen we call tarmac, asphalt or blacktop has served us pretty well for a century or so, but it is still vulnerable to the process of freeze-thaw weathering that creates potholes. The severe winter of 2009/10 reportedly left the UK with some 1.6 million potholes. Another consequence, thanks to all the loose chippings washing around, was a sudden shortage of replacement windscreens.

In the USA, where severe winter weather is standard issue, there are many unmetalled 'gravel roads' in rural areas. In some places, rather than being upgraded to 'blacktop', some roads are being returned to low-maintenance gravel in the interests of cost-cutting.

Another response to an alleged epidemic of potholes is to use them as art opportunities. In Britain, 'guerrilla gardeners' have taken to planting the holes with colourful flowers, while in New York they are fodder for conceptual artists who descend with props and in the space of a few minutes transform the ragged gap into a witty fantasy scene: an old woman washing clothes, a priest baptising a baby, a street vendor making doughnuts, even a peasant treading grapes into wine.

Fair Weather Fact

The chance of being struck by lightning is about
one in three million.

Well Said...

A lot of people like snow. I find it to be an unnecessary
freezing of water.

Carl Reiner, actor, film director, writer and comedian

Napoleon's Buttons

It is well known that Napoleon's biggest enemy when he
invaded Russia in 1812 was the weather. His Grande Armée
was reduced to a piteous rabble when the wretched troops,
inadequately equipped for Russian weather, froze to death in
their thousands in vicious sub-zero temperatures. If you
believe the story beloved of school chemistry teachers, this was
all to do with the different physical properties of the
allotropes of tin.

Pure tin is a brittle substance; a bar of it will break if you
bend it a few times. Indeed, as you bend it, you will feel and
even hear the crystal lattices in the metal shearing, producing

a screech of tortured atoms that is rather touchingly known as the 'tin cry'. Your bar actually contains two 'allotropes', or structural variants, of tin, just as pure carbon can exist in the form of diamond or graphite – and, as a comparison between pencils and wedding rings shows, the structure of crystal lattices is not always just a matter of mere academic interest. Two of the allotropes of tin are alpha-tin and beta-tin, commonly known as grey tin and white tin. White tin is the familiar metal, perfectly stable at room temperature, but in pure form it becomes unstable at temperatures below $13.2\,^\circ$C ($56\,^\circ$F); it becomes grey tin, which is a crumbly substance with no metallic properties. In practice, tin, a relatively expensive commodity, is not usually found in completely pure form, but contains traces of other metals such as zinc or aluminium, whose presence significantly lowers the temperature at which this disintegration starts to happen. Still, with prolonged exposure to sub-zero temperatures, tin objects will start to deteriorate, a process known as 'tin pest' or even, very graphically, as 'tin leprosy'. It happens over a long period, however, years or decades rather than weeks or months.

Well, according to the story – and you have a perfect right to believe it if you wish to – Napoleon's troops wore uniforms with buttons made of tin. In the freezing Russian winter, their buttons crumbled and fell off and the poor souls froze to death.

Les Nuages Qui Passent...

— *Eh ! qu'aimes-tu donc, extraordinaire étranger?*
— *J'aime les nuages ... les nuages qui passent ... là-bas ... là-bas ... les merveilleux nuages!*

– So what do you love, extraordinary stranger? – I love the clouds.
– The clouds that pass ... there ... there ... the wonderful clouds!

Charles Baudelaire, *'L'Etranger'*

International Weather Symbols: Ice

Ice crystals ('diamond dust')	↔
Ice pellets	△
Freezing drizzle	ᕼᴗ
Freezing rain	ᑯᴗ
Heavy icing	▲

Weatherphobias

The weather can be even scarier than you imagine...

- Clouds – nephophobia, nephelophobia
- Cold – psychrophobia
- Floods – antlophobia
- Fog – homichlophobia
- Freezing conditions – cryophobia, pagophobia
- Heat – thermophobia
- Lightning – astrapophobia
- Rain – pluviophobia, ombrophobia
- Severe storms – lilapsophobia
- Snow – chionophobia
- Sunshine – heliophobia
- Thunder – brontophobia, tonitrophobia
- Thunder and lightning – keraunophobia, ceraunophobia
- Waves – kymophobia, cymophobia
- Wind – ancraophobia, anemophobia

Well Said...

The weather is like the government, always in the wrong.

Jerome K. Jerome, writer and humorist

Snow Rollers

We can all picture the amazing natural sculptures the wind can create with sand, or even rock over the course of centuries. But not many of us have been lucky enough to witness a peculiar type of snow sculpture variously known as snow rollers, snow bales or even snow doughnuts.

In certain precise conditions, the wind can actually start the ball rolling, literally, or in even more freakish circumstances, given the impetus provided, say, by a lump of snow falling from a branch on to a downhill slope, mere gravity may do the job. Just like humans rolling a giant snowball along the ground to form the basis of a snowman, these lumps roll along, gathering bulk as they go, sometimes for surprising distances – diameters of 24in (61cm) have been claimed.

Any number of things could prevent this happening: the snow must be a particular kind of loose, wet snow, not too firm, not too powdery, and the ground must not be too sticky, so a layer of ice under the snow will help. The rollers tend to move in more or less straight lines, and the first tentative layers at the centre tend to melt away – like a ring doughnut.

But who would expect to find such a thing in the middle of a field of virgin snow with no human footprints in sight? And who knows what supernatural explanations may have sprung to mind in a more superstitious age.

Record Weather: Most Variable Temperature

The place with the greatest variations in temperature is Verkhoyansk in Siberia, where temperatures from -68 – 37°C (-90 to 99°F) have been recorded. At a place in Spearfish in South Dakota on 23 January 1948, the temperature rose from -20 to 7°C (-4 to 44°F); things went the other way at Browning, Montana, on 23–24 January 1916 when it fell from 7 to -49°C (44 to -56°F).

When to Visit ... San Francisco

July
Av. daily sunshine: 10 hrs
Av. monthly rainfall: ½in (17mm)
Av. max. temperature: 24°C (75.2°F)

SUMMER

Weather Words

Thirty days hath September
April, June and November
From January up to May
The rain it raineth every day
All the rest have thirty-one
Without a blessed gleam of sun
And if any of them had two-and-thirty
They'd be just as wet and twice as dirty.

Bill Giles, 'The Story of Weather'

Winds of the World: Part II

- **Khamseen, khamaseen, hamsin** – hot, dry, dusty wind of North Africa and the Arabian peninsula.
- **Khazri** – cold northerly coastal wind that blows across Baku.
- **Knik wind** – strong south-easterly wind in the Matanuska Valley of Alaska.
- **Koöava** – south-easterly wind that blows from the Carpathians into the Balkans.
- **Levant, levanter, llevant (Roussillon), levante (Corsica)** – moist easterly or north easterly wind in the Straits of Gibraltar and east coast of Spain and South of France.
- **Leveche, laveche, lebeche (Spain), llebeig (Catalonia), libeccio (Italy), leste (Madeira, Canaries)** – hot, dry, dusty south-westerly wind on Mediterranean coasts.

- **Loo** – hot, dry westerly summer wind that precedes the monsoon in Pakistan and northern India.
- **Marin** – warm, moist south-easterly wind blowing from the Mediterranean on to the south coast of France.
- **Matinal** – easterly 'morning' wind in the Massif Central of France.
- **Mistral, maestro, mistrau (Provence), mestral (Catalonia), maestrale (Italy)** – cold, dry north-westerly wind blowing down the Rhone Valley to the Mediterranean at anything up to 56mph (90km/h).
- **Nashi** – north-easterly winter wind in the Persian Gulf.
- **Ostro** – Italian name for the southerly wind of the Adriatic.
- **Pampero** – cold squally southerly or south-westerly wind blowing over the pampas of Argentina and Uruguay.
- **Purga, poorga (Russia), burga, boorga (Alaska)** – severe north-easterly storm in the tundra.
- **Santa Ana wind** – strong dry offshore wind blowing through southern California and northern Mexico.
- **Sarma** – strong, cold northerly wind blowing across Lake Baikal.
- **Shamal** – north-westerly wind blowing over Iraq and the Gulf states.
- **Simoom** – dry dusty wind in the Sahara, Levant or Arabian Peninsula.
- **Sirocco, scirocco, siroc, jaloque, xaloque (Spain), xaloc, xaloch (Catalonia), xaroco (Portugal)** – Mediterranean wind from the Sahara that can reach hurricane speeds.
- **Solano, solaire** – south-easterly or easterly wind on the southeast coast of Spain and southern France.
- **Squamish** – strong Arctic outflow wind in British Columbia.

- **Tehuantepecer** – strong, squally north-easterly mountain wind in the Gulf of Tehuantepec (southern Mexico), Nicaragua and Guatemala.
- **Tramontane (Provence), tramontana (Spain), tramuntana (Catalonia)** – strong cold, dry northerly wind blowing from the Massif Central.
- **Vardar, vardarac** – cold north-westerly wind that blows down the Vardar valley in Greece towards Thessaloniki.
- **Warm braw** – warm, dry wind during the monsoon in the Schouten Islands off New Guinea.
- **Williwaw, willywaw, willywau, willie-wa, willy-waa** – strong squall in the Straits of Magellan.
- **Willy-willy** – outdated term for a tropical cyclone of hurricane strength near Australia; also, a dust devil.
- **Zonda, sondo** – dry dusty wind blowing down the eastern sloes of the Andes; alternatively, a hot, humid northerly wind in the Pampas preceding the pampero.

Fair Weather Fact

The largest snowflake found to date was 15in (38cm) wide and 8in (20cm) thick. It fell at Fort Keogh, Montana, USA on 28 January 1887.

When to Visit ... Bangkok

December
Av. daily sunshine: 9 hrs
Av. monthly rainfall: ⅕in (5mm)
Av. max. temperature: 31°C (87.8°F)

Down the Sinkhole

The first named storm of the 2010 hurricane season was Tropical Storm Agatha. By the standards of tropical storms, this was a weak one, but catastrophic nevertheless. It made landfall on the Mexican–Guatemalan border, bringing torrential rain and disastrous mudslides. Worst hit was Guatemala, where over 100,000 people were evacuated and nearly 200 died. Weeks later, more than 100 were still missing. One of the most spectacular effects of the flooding was an enormous sinkhole at a street junction in a northern district of Guatemala City, which reputedly swallowed a three-storey clothing factory, leaving a hole 100ft (30.5m) deep. Locals blamed a crumbling sewage system and the damage caused by a constant traffic of heavy goods vehicles rumbling through the area.

Cloud Symbols: Middle Clouds

Middle clouds are found at 6,500–25,000ft (1,981–7,620m). These symbols are used by meteorologists for recording the types, combinations and development of clouds.

1. Thin, semi-transparent altostratus.

2. Thick altostratus or nimbostratus, hiding sun/moon.

3. Thin altocumulus, steady.

4. Thin altocumulus, patchy, shifting.

5. Thin altocumulus, patchy but spreading and thickening.

6. Altocumulus formed by spreading of cumulus or cumulonimbus.

7. Thick altocumulus, or with altostratus/nimbostratus.

8. Altocumulus with tufts or turrets (castellanus).

9. Multi-layer altocumulus, chaotic sky.

The Weather House

It is a quaint object, some might even say kitsch. A little model of an Alpine chalet, somewhat reminiscent of the casing of a cuckoo clock, with twin doors right and left, contains two little figures, one male, one female. The little man comes out, suitably equipped with an umbrella, to indicate rain; his good lady wife ventures out only in good weather, while he stays indoors, doubtless preserving his delicate skin from damaging ultra-violet.

This strange gadget is in fact no more or less than a hygrometer. At its heart is a simple piece of catgut or hair, which shrinks slightly when the air is dry and relaxes in wet weather, and the little figures swing back and forth on a little bar attached to this. No batteries are required, and this was one of the few household gadgets that was never in any danger from the millennium bug.

When to Visit ... Tokyo

July
Av. daily sunshine: 6 hrs
Av. monthly rainfall: 5½in (142mm)
Av. temperature: 28°C (82.4°F)

The Poet in Summer

I know I am but summer to your heart,
And not the full four seasons of the year;
And you must welcome from another part
Such noble moods as are not mine, my dear.
No gracious weight of golden fruits to sell
Have I, nor any wise and wintry thing;
And I have loved you all too long and well
To carry still the high sweet breast of spring.

Wherefore I say: O love, as summer goes,
I must be gone, steal forth with silent drums,
That you may hail anew the bird and rose
When I come back to you, as summer comes.
Else will you seek, at some not distant time,
Even your summer in another clime.

Edna St Vincent Millay, 'I Know I Am
But Summer to Your Heart'

A Joke For All Seasons

What did one hurricane say to the other hurricane?
I've got my eye on you.

Record Weather: Driest

The driest place in the world is famously the Atacama Desert in Chile where there is more or less no rainfall at all. A few times a century there is a passing shower, bumping up the annual average to a fraction of an inch, but decades pass without a drop falling.

Precipitation

Precipitation is, if you'll pardon the pun, an umbrella term for water that falls to earth in whatever form. There are a surprising number of different types including:

- **Drizzle** – strictly speaking, raindrops smaller than about $\frac{1}{50}$ in (0.5mm) are drizzle.
- **Freezing rain, freezing drizzle** – rain or drizzle that freezes when it hits a solid object, leaving a layer of glaze ice.

- **Hail** – defined as solid balls of ice between $\frac{1}{5}$in and (believe it or not) 6in (5–150mm).
- **Ice pellets, small hail** – small translucent balls of ice, smaller than hail.
- **Sleet** – in the UK, sleet refers to snow that melts as it falls, i.e. rain and snow mixed; however, in US parlance, it normally means ice pellets.
- **Snow pellets, soft hail, graupel** – formed when supercooled water freezes on to a snowflake to make a pellet about $\frac{1}{12}$–$\frac{1}{5}$in (2–5mm) across.
- **Snow grains, granular snow** – very small (under $\frac{1}{25}$in/1mm) grains of ice, like small solid drizzle, but falling in small quantities from stratus clouds or fog rather than a shower from a convective cloud.
- **Thundersnow** – snow rather than rain falling during a thunderstorm.

Well Said...

Sunshine is delicious, rain is refreshing, wind braces us, snow is exhilarating; there is really no such thing as bad weather, only different kinds of good weather.

John Ruskin (attributed), art critic, poet and social thinker

Jolly Boating Weather

The famous Eton School boat song was written in 1865 by the English poet and educationist William Cory (1823–1892). Famous perhaps, but who can quote more than that evocative first line? Typically of such songs, and in keeping with the public school ethos of the times, it emphasises the improving nature of teamwork, competitive sport and healthy outdoor exercise.

Jolly boating weather,
And a hay harvest breeze
Blade on the feather,
Shade off the trees.
Swing, swing together
With your backs between your knees.

Not surprisingly, it is this boating weather which serves to link the old Etonian to his schooldays for the rest of his life: the Proustian trigger that will make grown men sweltering in their offices wish they were once more schoolboys heaving together on an oar, on a gloriously sunny day of the sort that perhaps only exists in memory.

Twenty years hence this weather
May tempt us from office stools,
We may be slow on the feather,
And seem to the boys old fools,
But we'll still swing together
And swear by the best of schools.

Fair Weather Fact

The typical lifetime of a small cumulus cloud is between 10 and 15 minutes.

When to Visit ... The Maldives

January
Av. daily sunshine: 8 hrs
Av. monthly rainfall: 2in (46mm)
Av. max. temperature: 29°C (84.2°F)

Monsoon Health Tips

After the baking heat of summer in the Far East, you might think the monsoon would come as a blessed relief. The cooler temperatures are welcome, but the rain also increases the humidity. That humidity, along with riding floodwaters, brings a whole range of health problems. Water supplies become contaminated with groundwater and sewage. Water-borne and insect-carried diseases such as dengue, malaria and typhoid rise sharply, along with gastroenteritis and Hepatitis A. There is an increased risk of fungal infections of skin and nails. Food goes off more rapidly, especially when fridges stop working thanks to the frequent power-cuts. As usual when microbial infection is a risk, certain foods are best avoided: street snacks, especially anything including salad. Fruit and vegetables should be soaked in salt water to kill lurking insects, carefully washed and preferably steamed. *The Times of India* recommends a range of precautions which you might not have thought of: change out of wet clothes as soon as you can, and keep your feet dry; drink plenty of water and wash your hands often; avoid having stagnant water around the house, and change the water in vases daily. And 'wipe off the sweat and grime from your face and bathe often to feel cool and fresh'.

The Human Lightning Rod

Some are born great, some achieve greatness and some have greatness thrust upon them – or perhaps are struck by it. An American called Roy C. Sullivan (1912–1983) held the unenviable distinction of having survived more lightning strikes than any other human being known to recorded history. He was hit seven times, or possibly eight, and survived each time.

The first documented strike, and probably the worst, occurred in April 1942. Sullivan, who had started working as a ranger in the Shenandoah National Park in 1936, was in a fire-watching tower. Perhaps it was because the tower was newly built and no lightning conductor had yet been installed, but lightning struck the tower several times. 'Fire was jumping all over the place,' as Sullivan put it. Not surprisingly, he ran out, and a few feet away from the tower was hit by a bolt that 'burned a half-inch strip all the way down my right leg and knocked my big toe off.' You want more? 'My boot was full of blood, and it ran out through a hole in the sole.'

It's hard to imagine the horror of such an incident and one's feelings on having survived it. But then it happened again. In July 1969, Sullivan was driving along in his park-ranger's truck, when a bolt of lightning hit some trees on the left of the road, then jumped across to another tree on the right, apparently travelling straight through the vehicle passing between them. Even though the inside of a vehicle is normally a relatively safe place to be when lightning strikes, Sullivan lost all the hair up to the brim of his hat.

It happened again in July 1970. This time Sullivan was in his own garden when a power transformer was struck and the bolt jumped to his left shoulder. Was the poor man safe nowhere? Two years later he was working indoors when lightning hit the building. 'There was a gentle rain, but no thunder,' he reported, 'until just one big clap, the loudest thing I ever heard … When my ears stopped ringing, I heard something sizzling. It was my hair on fire.' Unable to get his head under the tap, Sullivan had to save what remained of his hair using wet paper towels.

By this time he was achieving a certain unwelcome notoriety as the 'Human Lightning Rod'. People would actively flee his company when the sky began to lower. Sullivan himself began to wonder whether he was presenting a danger to others by attracting the lightning in some mysterious way. Even the most rational man could be forgiven for becoming a little paranoid after his fourth lightning strike. He started to carry a can of water in his truck, and even began to think thunderclouds were following him.

And the water came in handy soon enough, when on 7 August 1973 he was 'followed' by a storm cloud. Thinking he had outrun it, he got out of the truck and was struck. Not for the first time, he was obliged to put out a fire in his own hair. It happened again, much the same way, on 5 June 1976. And yet again a year later, this time while he was fishing for trout. To add insult to injury, he then had to fight off a bear intent on stealing his catch.

Discounting the possibility that Sullivan was some kind of convincing liar – and his story, confirmed by the superintendent of Shenandoah National Park, was good enough for the *Guinness Book of Records* – it is a tale that stretches belief in coincidence to the limit. A human being does not 'attract' lightning, surely, not more than any other comparable human being. So what, as they say, are the chances?

The Great Storm: Part II

Michael Fish's comment during his weather report on the eve of the 'Great Storm of 1987' that there wasn't in fact a hurricane heading to the UK has been endlessly quoted down the years. However, his statement related not to the forecast for the UK at this point, but instead to a story that had featured in the news, concerning a different hurricane that was centred around Florida and the Caribbean. The comment he did make regarding the UK forecast was 'batten down the hatches there's some really stormy weather on the way', but this has gone largely ignored.

Sunshine on a Cloudy Day

During the day the amount of sunshine reaching the ground depends on the amount of cloud cover. The amount of cloud cover is usually given in units called 'oktas', and each okta represents ⅛th of the sky covered by cloud.

- Clear sky
- One okta
- Two oktas
- Three oktas
- Four oktas
- Five oktas
- Six oktas
- Seven oktas
- Eight oktas: completely overcast
- Sky obscured

An easy way to measure cloud cover is to use a large mirror divided into 16 equal squares using a dark crayon. Lay the mirror on the ground somewhere the whole sky is visible, and then count the squares or parts of squares with cloud in them. Divide that number by two to convert sixteenths into oktas.

The Beatles' Top 10
(Outlook positive)

1. 'Here Comes the Sun'
2. 'Good Day Sunshine'
3. 'Mother Nature's Son'
4. 'I'll Follow the Sun'
5. 'Sun King'
6. 'Lucy in the Sky with Diamonds'
7. 'The Inner Light'
8. 'Watching Rainbows' (unreleased)
9. 'Carnival of Light'
10. 'Rain'

Well Said...

One swallow does not make a summer, neither does one fine day; similarly one day or brief time of happiness does not make a person entirely happy.

Aristotle, philosopher

Record Weather: Sunniest

The annual average sunshine total in the eastern Sahara is around 4,300 hours, which represents some 97% of the total possible. Meanwhile, the South Pole receives only 182 sunny days a year.

Summer Reading

Northern Lights (1995)	Philip Pullman
The Rainbow (1915)	D. H. Lawrence
Light in August (1932)	William Faulkner
A Man for All Seasons (1954)	Robert Bolt
Middlemarch (1874)	George Eliot
The Moonstone (1868)	Wilkie Collins
The Sun Also Rises (1926)	Ernest Hemingway
A High Wind in Jamaica (1929)	Richard Hughes
The Old Man and the Sea (1952)	Ernest Hemingway
Raisin in the Sun (1959)	Lorraine Hansberry
Wind, Sand and Stars (1939)	Antoine de Saint Exupery
King of the Wind (1948)	Marguerite Henry
The Wind in the Willows (1908)	Kenneth Grahame
If On A Winter's Night A Traveller (1979)	Italo Calvino
Gone with the Wind (1936)	Margaret Mitchell
The Hurricane (1936)	Charles Nordhoff & James Hall
From the Earth to the Moon (1870)	Jules Verne

William on Weather: Part II

You and you no cross shall part;
You and you are heart in heart;
You to his love must accord,
Or have a woman to your lord;
You and you are sure together,
As the winter to foul weather.
The Comedy of Errors

A tree whose boughs did bend with fruit; but in one night
A storm, or robbery, call it what you will,
Shook down my mellow hangings, nay, my leaves,
And left me bare to weather
Cymbeline

But I with blowing the fire shall warm myself; for, considering
the weather, a taller man than I will take cold.
The Taming of the Shrew

[A cry within] A plague upon this howling! They are louder
than the weather or our office.
The Tempest

Was this a face
To be opposed against the jarring winds?
To stand against the deep dread-bolted thunder?
In the most terrible and nimble stroke
Of quick, cross lightning?
King Lear

Our gayness and our gilt are all besmirch'd
With rainy marching in the painful field
Henry V

Like a red morn that ever yet betokened,
Wreck to the seaman, tempest to the field,
Sorrow to the shepherds, woe unto the birds,
Gusts and foul flaws to herdmen and to herds.
Venus and Adonis

When to Visit ... Bombay

February
Av. daily sunshine: 10 hrs
Av. monthly rainfall: ¹/₁₀in (3mm)
Av. max. temperature: 28°C (82.4°F)

The Saffir-Simpson Hurricane Scale

Hurricanes are graded on a scale devised in the early 1970s by Herbert Saffir and Robert Simpson, evaluating potential damage based on wind speed and storm surge. A hurricane technically qualifies as such when its wind speed reaches 64 knots (74mph, 119km/h). Strictly speaking, the word hurricane can only be applied to storms forming in the Atlantic Ocean and northern Pacific Ocean east of the International Date Line. Lower wind speeds (34–63 knots, 39–73mph) are defined as a tropical storm.

Category	Pressure (hectopascals)	Wind speed (knots/mph /km/h)	Storm surge (ft/m)	Damage
1	980	64–82/74–95/ 119–153	4–5/ 1.2–1.5	Minimal
2	965–980	83–95/96–110/ 155–177	6–8/ 1.8–2.4	Moderate
3	111–130	6–113/111– 130/179–209	9–12/ 2.7–3.7	Extensive
4	131–155	114–134/131– 155/211–250	13–18/ 4–5.5	Extreme
5	-155	135+/156+/251+	18+/5.5+	Catastrophic

Inside a Thundercloud

What child has not wondered what the inside of a cloud would be like? Flying through them aboard a jet plane is a big letdown – just a whiteout of freezing mist. But a few rare individuals have had the personal experience of flying or falling through a cloud, without the protection of a metal fuselage, and that experience is not to be recommended to anyone.

On Valentine's Day 2007, a group of some 200 paragliders were training for the World Championships in New South Wales. Two of them were swept into a giant cumulonimbus storm cloud, a phenomenon known as cloud suck. This is dangerous for all kinds of aircraft – even jumbo jets avoid these 'storm cells' with their powerful updrafts, hailstones and electrical discharges – but for a paraglider, who has no more than a parachute with a good sense of direction and a maximum speed of less than 30 knots (35mph/56km/h), they are lethal. Temperatures can be as low as -40°C/F and the air currents are so powerful that, even without a canopy, a human being is powerless to fall out of the cloud. And of course at those altitudes there is very little oxygen, and paragliders carry no breathing apparatus.

One of the cloud's victims was later found, frozen to death, many miles away from the launch site. The other was Ewa Wisnierska, a 35-year-old Polish woman based in Germany. By a truly freakish piece of luck, she escaped almost unscathed. Not long after entering the cloud, she blacked out due to lack of oxygen, and this may have been what saved her life, by slowing her vital functions to a minimum. According to data recovered from her altimeter and GPS unit, she had been swept up at a rate of 66ft/sec (20m/sec) to an altitude of over 32,000ft (9,754m), the cruising height of jet airliners.

'After about 40 minutes, I woke up,' she said. 'Everything was frozen ... I scratched the GPS and I was at 6,900m [22,632ft] and I was still flying.' She sustained bruising from hailstones and some frostbite, but three and a half hours after taking off she managed to land safely. Wisnierska is still an active paraglider, and one of very few human beings to have fallen through a thundercloud, and lived to tell the tale.

Under the Weather: Part II
(Weather clichés for fair weather friends)

· Got your head in the clouds
· One man's foul weather is another man's fair
· Not a snowball's chance in hell
· Once in a blue moon
· Pure as the driven snow
· The quiet before the storm
· Run like the wind
· Sail into the sunset
· Skating on thin ice

Fair Weather Fact

One inch (2.5cm) of rainwater is equivalent to 15in (30cm)
of dry, powdery snow.

A Joke For All Seasons

Where does a meteorologist stop for a drink after a long day?
The nearest isobar.

The Poet in Autumn

Coldly, sadly descends
The autumn-evening. The field
Strewn with its dank yellow drifts
Of witheríd leaves, and the elms,
Fade into dimness apace,
Silent; – hardly a shout
From a few boys late at their play!

Matthew Arnold, 'Rugby Chapel', November 1857

Contrails and Distrails

The impact of human activity is visible everywhere on earth. Footprints in what we thought were virgin snows, tyre-tracks in the desert sand, show us we are not the first to pass this way. Human beings are everywhere and leave traces of their passage. But for the most part the sky above us is unsullied; it's possible to lie on your back and stare up at the blue expanse and picture yourself a thousand or a million years ago. Unless you live under a flight path of course.

Even if there are no aircraft in the sky, we can often see where they have been. What exactly causes these white streaks that criss-cross the sky, like chalk-marks on a blackboard? Like the wake of a boat, they eventually fade away, but these are not wakes. Nor is it clouds of sooty particles like the visible exhaust of a badly maintained motor vehicle that we can see. It's really just condensation. Aircraft too burn fuel made of hydrocarbons, but the main products are carbon dioxide and water. These white streaks – perhaps they resemble the score-makers left by skaters on ice – are known as condensation trails or 'contrails'.

As we know, when air is warmer (or drier) it can hold more water. The water emerges from a hot aircraft engine in the form of invisible vapour, but of course the sky is a cold place at the altitudes where airliners are found – 5 miles (8km) up, the temperature might be -40°C or lower. So the water cools rapidly on contact with the air and condenses into droplets, which freeze into ice crystals. They may form around exhaust particles like the ones that come out of a car engine, but of course these particles are far too small to be visible, so contrails look snowy white. In dry air contrails are less likely to form than in moist air, or will form but not spread, and will dissipate more rapidly than in moist air.

Strange how cars seem like much worse polluters on a freezing-cold day, when they trail clouds of white exhaust behind them: not fumes, just steam.

But it's not just the engines that leave contrails: you can see them flowing from the wingtips of the plane, or from the lowered flaps as the plane lands. Unlike cars, aircraft can cause condensation in another way; simply by passing through the air they can cause the water already present in the air to condense. There is a clue to this in the swirling pattern often observable in contrails. What enables an aircraft to rise through the air is the specially designed shape of its wings, the 'aerofoil', which causes air above the wing to travel faster and hence lowers its pressure relative to the air below the wing. At the tips and sometimes the trailing edge of the wings, the air has a tendency to wrap back up and over, causing 'wingtip vortices'. Temperature and pressure being linked by the laws of physics, the lower-pressure air, which is to say cooler air, is another possible site of condensation, and it shows up in visible swirls. Contrails can be produced by propeller-driven aircraft just as much as by jets, and there it is sometimes possible to see loops of condensation caused by the whirling propellers.

But as we've noted, everything depends on the temperature and humidity of the air the plane passes through. What if it is already full of vapour? What we ordinary people might call a 'cloud', in fact. Well, a plane can cut a kind of tunnel of clear air through it. The hot exhaust gases can warm the air enough to cause the condensation in it to be re-absorbed, leaving a trail free of condensation: the opposite of a contrail, if you like. This is known as a dissipation trail, or 'distrail'.

The Naming of Clouds
(non-scientific)

Here are some cloud names that are not part of the formally accepted 'scientific' system of nomenclature:

- **Anvil cloud** – cumulonimbus incus, the distinctive flat-topped cloud that heralds thunderstorms.
- **Banner cloud** – a triangular plume of cloud extending sideways from the peak of a mountain.
- **Breast cloud** – mammatus or mammatocumulus, with 'udders' hanging under its base.
- **Cap cloud, scarf cloud** – English name for the 'pileus' or little extra cloud that sometimes appears above a cumulus or cumulonimbus.
- **Cauliflower cloud, woolpack cloud** – cumulus, the 'fair weather' cloud.
- **Fallstreaks, virga** – wisps of ice crystals that fall away from cirrus clouds as they accumulate and grow heavier.
- **Fumulus** – cumulus cloud caused by the moisture rising from industrial sources such as smokestacks and cooling towers.
- **Mare's tails, goat's hair, hen feathers, spider webs** – all names for cirrus.
- **Nacreous cloud, mother of pearl cloud** – more technically known as polar stratospheric clouds, these are found at altitudes of 50,000–80,000ft (15,240–24,384m).
- **Noctilucent clouds** – thin silver-blue wisps seen in the summer at high latitudes; the highest visible clouds, 250,000–275,000ft (76,200–83,820m) above the Earth.

- **Pile d'assiettes ('pile of plates')** – a stack of disc-shaped lenticular clouds; apparently the only internationally accepted cloud term in French rather than Latin.
- **Pyrocumulus** – cumulus cloud caused by hot air rising from a volcano or large fire.
- **Thunderhead** – the 'anvil' or upper part of a cumulonimbus cloud.
- **Water dog, water bearer** – a cloud supposed to indicate rain.

The Kite

The kite may be a toy most of the time but it has had many practical applications too. In meteorology it has been invaluable. Benjamin Franklin, in his fabled experiments with lightning, is often fancifully depicted flying a kite into a thunderstorm with a key jumping and fizzing on the string: a good stunt for any scientist tired of life. A kite is also a simple and effective way of placing anything up in the air without a supporting structure – a matter of allowing the wind to lift it, rather than pushing it up on a pole. Now, meteorologists at Reading University are pioneering a method of using a rokkaku (Japanese fighting kite) to measure wind strength using strain gauges at the base of the tether, which offers 'an easily implemented method for investigating lower atmosphere air flows, such as those which transport pollution'.

In Case of an Emergency ...

Excessive water or wind, or both at once, can cause major headaches for the householder. After fire, a flood is the most destructive element that can hit your home.

Ready supplies

It may be worthwhile having a supply of tinned and dried food and bottled water in case you are cut off for any length of time. It may also be useful to buy a camping light, camping cooker and candles, as the first thing you'll have to do in a flood is turn off the mains electricity.

If you have room in a garage or shed, keep a stock of plastic bags filled with sand or soil to block off outside doors and airbricks.

Be prepared

Even if a downpour looks as though it is going to turn into a flood, you should have a reasonable amount of time to prepare the house and your family.

- Block off outside doors and airbricks to try to keep water out of the house; place plastic carrier bags filled with soil against the outside faces of doors and airbricks.
- Turn off mains electricity, gas and water.
- Move your family, pets and what possessions you can (furniture, rugs, etc.) to upper floors, or move out if in a bungalow.
- Take off downstairs internal doors, if possible. Severe flooding may damage them.
- Wait upstairs for the relief services to tell you what to do next.

Cleaning up after a flood

Let the emergency services pump as much water out of the house as possible before trying to return. Once back inside, check the damage very carefully.

- If water has got into the electrics, it could be dangerous and you should get the local electricity company to test it as soon as possible. All appliances should also be examined and tested at the same time.
- Call in the local gas suppliers to check the system and any appliances.
- Check with the water company on the state of the water supplies.
- You should be able to hire a pump to clear any remaining water from cellars, and then use a three-in-one vacuum cleaner to remove any final pools of water.
- Check the loft for any damage. It may need temporary repairs to stop the roof letting in even more water. An uncovered water cistern in the loft may be contaminated and so you'll need to drain it and clean it out. Throw out soaked loft insulation material.
- Remove furniture and lift floor coverings so you can hose walls and floors down. Scrub all affected surfaces thoroughly with strong disinfectant, as the floodwater may have been contaminated with sewage.
- If you didn't get a chance to do this before the flood, take doors off their hinges and stack them flat so they can dry out without warping.
- Lift some floorboards so the underfloor area can dry out or be pumped out if necessary.
- Check that there is no water trapped underneath ground floors, in cellars or cavity walls. If water has got inside them, holes may have to be drilled from the outside to allow it to escape. Also check for trapped mud.

- Outside, make sure airbricks are free of debris. Unblock drains, clean out gully gratings and rod the drains to clear them.
- Keep windows and doors open as often as possible (security permitting) to give good ventilation, even when the heating is on. Good ventilation is crucial. Your greatest enemy is rotting timber.
- At night, you could use a dehumidifier (which removes moisture from the air and collects it in a container which you then empty). When you think the structural and joinery timbers are dry, call in a surveyor to check the moisture content.
- If the wallpaper is ruined, strip it off to help speed up drying out. Leave cupboard doors open and keep furniture away from walls.
- If walls are very damp, it may be necessary to have some of the inside plaster removed to aid drying out.

When to Visit ... Cairo

April
Av. daily sunshine: 10 hrs
Av. monthly rainfall: 1/25in (1mm)
Av. max. temperature: 28°C (82.4°F)

Top 10 British Weather Disasters: Part II

6. The 1976 Drought: During this year, a long, hot summer combined with a prolonged period of low rainfall caused a severe drought and provided ideal conditions for devastating heathland and forest fires. In parts of Dorset and Devon there was no rain for 45 continuous days. In June the temperature topped 32°C (89.6°F) for 14 days in a row.

7. The Great Storm of 1987: An area of low pressure caused high winds that battered the south coast of England during the night of 15 October 1987. The strongest gust over the UK was 122mph (196km/h) at Gorleston, Norfolk. There were 19 deaths and the storm caused an estimated £1bn of damage. The winds were accompanied by huge changes in temperature as the storm passed. At Farnborough in Hampshire, the temperature rose from 8.5°C (47.3°F) to 17.6°C (63.7°F) in 20 minutes.

8. The Spring Snowstorm of 1908: On 25 April 1908 snow began to fall over Berkshire, Oxfordshire, Buckinghamshire and Hampshire. By the time the blizzard ended, the snow was 2ft (61cm) deep. Temperatures on the north of Scotland fell to as low as -12.8°C (9°F).

9. The Boscastle Floods of 2004: A flash flood in the north Cornwall village of Boscastle caused devastation on 16 August 2004. A torrent of water 10ft (3m) high surged through the village when 3in (77mm) of rain fell in just two hours. It was estimated that two million tons (440 million gallons/2 billion litres) of water rushed through the village, causing extensive damage to property and vehicles. However, no one was killed or seriously injured during the floods.

10. The Winter of 1963: One of the coldest winters on record – snow began to fall on Boxing Day 1962 and much of the country remained covered until March 1963. During the long cold spell, lakes and rivers froze and even some harbours turned to ice. By the time the thaw finally arrived, the winter had been the coldest for 200 years.

Record Weather: Coldest

No surprises here: the winner is Antarctica. The Pole of Inaccessibility has an annual average temperature of -57.8°C (-72°F). The lowest ever recorded temperature was at Vostok Station on 21 July 1983 with -89.2°C (-128.6°F). The lowest temperature for a permanently inhabited place is Oymyakon in Siberia with a claimed -72°C (-98°F).

AUTUMN

METAR Codes

METAR is a set of standard conventions for reporting weather, introduced in 1968 and standardised by the International Civil Aviation Organization (ICAO) and used primarily by pilots and forecasters. The name is said to be derived from the French phrase 'message d'observation météorologique pour l'aviation régulière'. Here are some of its abbreviations for different hazards:

DZ: drizzle
FC: funnel cloud
FG: fog
FU: smoke
GR: hail
HZ: haze
IC: ice crystals
PL: ice pellets
PO: dust/sand whirls (dust devils)
PY: spray (on runways)
RA: rain
SG: snow grains
SN: snow
SP: snow pellets
SQ: squalls
SS: sandstorm
TS: thunderstorm
VA: volcanic ash

A Flash of Inspiration

A certain mythology surrounds the life of Benjamin Franklin (1706–1790). We perhaps know him best as an early American statesman and political theorist, but he was also a scientist, who did much valuable research into electricity.

In June 1752, Franklin made the following observation: during a thunderstorm, the loose fibres on a kite line, soaked by the rain, would bristle up instead of being slicked down, and that, if he brought his hand towards a key attached to the end of the line, a spark would jump across the gap. No one quite knows why Franklin was out flying a kite in a storm – he may have been trying to prove the build-up of electricity in the air during the course of the storm – but his point was that lightning was caused by the build-up of large amounts of electricity in the atmosphere.

Franklin was not the first to attempt to find ways to protect buildings from the destructive power of lightning. The term 'lightning conductor' implies something designed to carry a lightning strike safely away to earth, and this it must be able to do, Franklin noted, by being sufficiently heavy-duty to withstand millions of volts and tens of thousands of degrees centigrade – a temperature several times hotter than the surface of the sun. Tall buildings will suffer repeated strikes: for example, during one storm, the Empire State Building was hit 15 times in as many minutes. There are supposedly about 100 lightning flashes every second somewhere in the world, which would translate into 8 million every day.

But the principal aim of a lightning conductor, or lightning rod as they are known in the United States, is to prevent the lightning strike ever happening in the first place by 'defusing' the build-up of charge that causes it. There was much debate at first over whether this was best done by a rod ending in a round ball, or one where the tip (what is known as the air terminal or lightning finial) ends in a sharp point, which some argued would 'invite' the lightning. Franklin's sharp points eventually won, but he had other specifications too: a stout rod with carefully soldered junctions, sunk at least 10ft (3m) into the earth, with its base several feet away from the building to protect the foundations, if possible earthed to a nearby well, and protected against corrosion by a coat of paint. To this da,y no one has come up with any substantial improvement on this idea.

Astrapophobia

The fear of lightning is one of the most distressing infirmities a human being can be afflicted with. It is mostly confined to women; but now and then you find it in a little dog, and sometimes in a man. It is a particularly distressing infirmity, for the reason that it takes the sand out of a person to an extent, which no other fear can, and it can't be reasoned with, and neither can it be shamed out of a person. A woman who could face the very devil himself – or a mouse – loses her grip and goes all to pieces in front of a flash of lightning. Her fright is something pitiful to see.

Mark Twain, *Mrs McWilliams and the Lightning*

Seasonal Recipes
Autumn Vegetable Soup

Preparation Time 15 minutes · Cooking Time 45 minutes · Serves 4 · Per Serving 326 calories, 17g fat (of which 9g saturates), 29g carbohydrate, 1.1g salt

2oz (50g) butter
1 medium onion, diced
1lb (450g) potatoes, diced
3½oz (100g) diced bacon
1 garlic clove, chopped
3½oz (100g) white of leek, chopped
2 Cox's Orange Pippin apples, unpeeled, cored and chopped
2 tsp dried thyme
1 tsp dill seeds (optional)
1 pint (600ml) dry cider
1½ pints (900ml) hot vegetable stock
4oz (125g) Savoy cabbage leaves, shredded
Salt and ground black pepper

1   Melt the butter in a large pan, then add the onion, potatoes, bacon, garlic, leek, apples, thyme and dill seeds if using. Season to taste with salt and pepper, stir, then cover and cook gently for 15 minutes.

2   Add the cider and bring to the boil, then reduce the heat and simmer for five minutes. Add the hot stock and simmer for about 15 minutes or until the potatoes are soft.

3 Pour half the soup into a blender or liquidiser and whizz
   until smooth. Add to the remaining soup in the pan.
   Reheat gently, add the shredded cabbage and simmer for
   a further three minutes.

The Cloud Appreciation Society

The Cloud Appreciation Society was founded in 2004 by
Gavin Pretor-Pinney, 'as a bit of a joke'. A designer by trade,
he is also co-founder of *The Idler* magazine, and describes
himself as 'not a scientist or a meteorologist or anything like
that … just someone who loves clouds'. The Society now
claims about 22,000 members in some 82 different
countries. Its 'manifesto' is reminiscent of the words of Luke
Howard, to whom the sky 'can never be to the zealous
Naturalist a subject of tame and unfeeling contemplation'.
Why should a serious interest in a natural phenomenon
preclude the sort of poetic imagination that sees shapes in the
sky? 'Clouds are for dreamers,' the cloudheads tell us, 'and
their contemplation benefits the soul. Indeed, all who
consider the shapes they see in them will save on
psychoanalysis bills.'

Significant Others:
Heroes of Weather

- Luke Howard – 'The Man Who Named The Clouds'
- St Swithin – 'The Weather Saint'
- JMW Turner – 'The Painter of Light'
- William Shakespeare – 'The Bard'
- Michael 'Hurricane' Fish – creator of the 'Michael Fish Effect'

When to Visit ... Buenos Aires

November
Av. daily sunshine: 9 hrs
Av. monthly rainfall: $3\frac{1}{4}$in (84mm)
Av. max. temperature: 24°C (75.2°F)

Watermelon Snow

Never eat the yellow snow, they say. But watermelon snow sounds quite appetising, in fact almost culinary, perhaps something you might find adorning an upmarket dessert. Chlamydomonas nivalis sounds less appealing, more medical perhaps. But that's the 'green' algae that gives watermelon snow its strange pinkish tint. It's a red 'green' algae, you see, green in the sense that it's chlorophyll-based like a very primitive plant, but actually coloured red due to the presence of astaxanthin, which is found in such pinkish creatures as salmon, lobsters and prawns, as well as the feathers of flamingos. Apparently, the red pigment protects the chloroplast, the part of the cell that produces energy by photosynthesis, from the damaging effects of too much ultraviolet light. It also helps it absorb heat, which melts the surrounding snow slightly and supplies this unicellular organism with water.

The result is that, in certain parts of the world above about 10,000ft (3,048m), the snow can take on a pinkish or even downright bloody tinge which must be quite startling to those not used to it. Walking on this snow compresses the algae and leaves a bright watermelon-red footprint, as well as red marks on your footwear and clothing. It can even have a slight odour of watermelon. The red pigment typically appears in streaks on the snow, which can look disturbingly like streams of blood.

The expedition led by Captain John Ross in 1818 to find the North-west Passage encountered this puzzling red snow and brought back samples. The August edition of *The Times* was rocked on its heels: 'Our credulity is put to an extreme test upon this occasion, but we cannot learn that there is any reason to doubt the fact as stated … The liquor, or dissolved snow, is of so dark a red as to resemble red port wine.' At the time it was put down to the presence of iron, 'the colourist of all metallic as well as vegetable matter'.

Lost in Translation

Weather names of wonder.

Aputsiaq: little snowflake, in Greenland
Bourkan: volcano, in Arabic
Dumisa: causes thunder, in African Zulu
Edur: snow, in Basque
Feng: galloping horse or wind, in Chinese
Glaw: rain, in Welsh
Hung: flood, in Chinese
Lei: thunder, in Chinese
Lokni: rain, in Native American Miwok
Makani: wind, in Hawaiian
Nasim: breeze, in Arabic
Raiden: thunder, in Japanese
Shant: thunderbolt, in Armenian
Vanada: rain-giver, in Hindi
Yas: snow, in Native American Navajo
Zephyrus: west wind, in Latin

The Months

January brings the snow,
Makes our feet and fingers glow.

February brings the rain,
Thaws the frozen lake again.

March brings breezes loud and shrill,
Stirs the dancing daffodil.

April brings the primrose sweet,
Scatters daisies at our feet.

May brings flocks of pretty lambs,
Skipping by their fleecy damns.

June brings tulips, lilies, roses,
Fills the children's hands with posies.

Hot **July** brings cooling showers,
Apricots and gillyflowers.

August brings the sheaves of corn,
Then the harvest home is borne.

Warm **September** brings the fruit,
Sportsmen then begin to shoot.

Fresh **October** brings the pheasant,
Then to gather nuts is pleasant.

Dull **November** brings the blast,
Then the leaves are whirling fast.

Chill **December** brings the sleet,
Blazing fire, and Christmas treat.

Sara Coleridge *(daughter of Samuel Taylor Coleridge)*

Fair Weather Fact

The angle of light refraction required to create a rainbow is 42° from the eye of the observer.

Weather Cocktails: Part III

Golden Dawn	Gin, orange juice, lemon juice, apricot brandy, grenadine.
Tropical Sun	Gin, passion-fruit syrup, lemon juice, tropical bitter (or soda), grenadine, slice of orange, maraschino cherry.
Seven Seas	Pisang Ambon, gin, crème de banane, tonic water, 1 maraschino cherry.
Red Sunshine	Gin, blackcurrant-flavoured liquer, lemon juice, soda water.
Windjammer	Light rum, dry vermouth, grenadine, 2 maraschino cherries.
Snow White	Light rum, lemon juice, pineapple juice, sugar syrup, 1 egg white.
Lovely Rainbow	Drambuie, orange juice, lemon juice, grenadine, slice of orange, slice of lemon.
Snowball	Advocaat, lemonade.

When to Visit ... Marrakech

May
Av. daily sunshine: 9 hrs
Av. monthly rainfall: ¾in (20mm)
Av. max. temperature: 29°C (84.2°F))

Useful Metaphors: In Conversation

The police *froze* their bank accounts!
Hopefully it'll be *clear skies* from now on.
Let us bid them all a *warm* welcome!
He thinks we have a *stormy* relationship.

Fair Weather Fact

The highest natural surface wind velocity ever recorded – an
incredible 231mph – was at Mt Washington, New
Hampshire, USA on April 12th 1934.

Cloud symbols: Low Clouds

Low clouds are found below 6,500ft (1,981m). These symbols are used by meteorologists for recording the types, combinations and development of clouds.

1. Fair-weather cumulus,
   little vertical development.

2. Towering cumulus (congestus).

3. Cumulonimbus, tops not
   fibrous (cirriform) or
   anvil-shaped (calvus).

4. Stratocumulus formed by
   spreading of cumulus, often
   also cumulus.

5. Stratocumulus not formed
   by spreading of cumulus.

6. Stratus, continuous layers.

7. Foul-weather stratus, often
   with nimbostratus.

8. Cumulus and stratocumulus
   with bases at different levels.

9. Cumulonimbus with tops
   clearly fibrous/anvil-shaped (incus).

Napoleon's Wallpaper

Weather has had many strange effects on the course of human history, but rarely have circumstances come together in such an unpredictable way as in the singular case of Napoleon's wallpaper.

As every schoolboy used to know, in the days when the phrase 'as every schoolboy knows' was in common currency, Napoleon Bonaparte ended his days on the remote volcanic island of St Helena in the South Atlantic, a good 1,000 miles (1,609km) from any major landfall. He had been exiled there by the British authorities in October 1815, having met his Waterloo. His health started to fail, rather suddenly, in February 1821, and he died in May of that year. He was buried on the island, and not until 1840 were his remains disinterred and sent back to France for a state funeral.

But how exactly did Boney die? The mystery has never been cleared up to everyone's satisfaction. The autopsy conducted by his personal physician found evidence of a stomach ulcer, and the cause of death was put down to stomach cancer. Stomach cancer is still a perfectly credible possibility, but in the second half of the 20th century, following the publication of the diaries of Napoleon's valet, theories began to circulate that he had died of poisoning, perhaps by cyanide, perhaps mercury, but more likely arsenic. This might explain the excellent state of preservation of his remains when removed from the island in 1840.

Arsenic accumulates in the body and has been easily detectable ever since the invention of a reliable test by the British chemist James Marsh in 1836. It had previously been a popular choice of poison by those who had, shall we say, grown tired of their spouses, gaining the macabre nickname 'poudre de succession' ('inheritance powder'); the most notorious case of an alleged arsenical murderer was perhaps Marie-Fortunèe Lafarge, who (rightly or wrongly) was convicted of dispatching her husband by this method, in the very same year that Napoleon's mortal remains were exhumed and repatriated. Traces of arsenic can often be found in the victim's hair, and, thanks to the tradition of keeping a lock or two as a keepsake or souvenir, samples of Napoleon's hair do still exist, passed down by those who had been around him in his last days. Sure enough, they show a very high level of arsenic, many times above normal, very possibly enough to kill him.

But what was the nature of his death, if indeed he was killed by arsenic? Was he murdered, or did he succumb accidentally? We will probably never know for sure. Some claim the substance was administered as a poison, and indeed various parties could be said to have had a motive, not least the British authorities. However, the fact is that in the 19th century arsenic was used commercially in a wide range of domestic products such as dyes and insecticides. The key to Napoleon's death could lie in, of all things, the colour of his wallpaper. If his rooms at Longwood House had been decorated with a bright-green paper, this would very probably have contained commonly used dyes such as Paris green or Scheele's Green. These dyes are safe enough in normal room conditions, given that most people do not try to eat their wallpaper, but if the paper is allowed to become damp and mouldy, a strange natural process can take place: the mould excretes the arsenic in gaseous form into the air. Breathing in too much of this vapour can cause a form of poisoning known as Gosio's disease.

The question of the colour of Napoleon's wallpaper was the missing link in this accidental poisoning theory, until by a remarkable stroke of luck, a sample of it showed up a few years ago in a scrap-book in private hands in Norfolk. Sure enough, the paper was green, with a pattern of gold stars. Not only are green and gold the imperial colours, but the pattern is confirmed by close examination of contemporary pictures of the interior of Longwood House. But could he have breathed in enough airborne arsenic to receive a fatal dose? And what has all this got to do with the weather, anyway?

The climate of St Helena, a tropical island swept by humid trade winds, is warm and wet, and damp walls may well have been a feature of the emperor's apartments. But even so, it would probably have been difficult to absorb a high enough dose, in normal circumstances. And yet, there is still one tantalising possibility. Apparently, Napoleon was given to taking bracing walks around the island, and even took up gardening. But during periods of illness, he would naturally spend more time shut up in his room, increasing his exposure to the cumulative toxin which might or might not have been ruining his health in the first place. Was the Emperor of the French, in fact, killed by his wallpaper? Or in some sense, by the weather?

The Poet in Autumn

Season of mists and mellow fruitfulness!
Close bosom-friend of the maturing sun;
Conspiring with him how to load and bless
With fruit the vines that round the thatch-eaves run;
To bend with apples the moss'd cottage trees,
And fill all fruit with ripeness to the core.

John Keats, 'To Autumn'

Well Said...

I've lived in good climate, and it bores the hell out of me. I like weather rather than climate.

John Steinbeck, author

Fair Weather Fact

The tiny droplets of water that make up fog are so small that it would take seven thousand million of them to make a single tablespoonful of water.

Weather-related Street Names: Cardiff

• **Clearwater Way** • **Coldstream Terrace** • **Dew Crescent** • **Dryden Close** • **Fairwater Avenue** • **Newgale Place** • **Sun Street** • **Wyndham Road**

The Weather in New England

Mark Twain, ever the wit and raconteur, once lectured the New England Society, at their 71st Annual Dinner on 22 December 1876, on the subject of the weather in New England. He decided that the weather there must be manufactured by trainees who had yet to master the art, who hoped to graduate to places where the clientele is fussier:

'I reverently believe that the Maker who made us all makes everything in New England but the weather. I don't know who makes that, but I think it must be raw apprentices in the weather-clerk's factory who experiment and learn how, in New England, for board and clothes, and then are promoted to make weather for countries that require a good article, and will take their custom elsewhere if they don't get it.'

New England just has to put up with what it gets, like a free student haircut. But it certainly gains in variety and novelty:

'There is a sumptuous variety about the New England weather that compels the stranger's admiration – and regret. The weather is always doing something there; always attending strictly to business; always getting up new designs and trying them on the people to see how they will go. But it gets through more business in spring than in any other season.

'In the spring I have counted one hundred and thirty-six different kinds of weather inside of four-and-twenty hours. It was I that made the fame and fortune of that man that had that marvelous collection of weather on exhibition at the Centennial, that so astounded the foreigners. He was going to travel all over the world and get specimens from all the climes.

I said, 'Don't you do it; you come to New England on a favorable spring day.'

Residents of the Old England will doubtless say he might equally have been talking about their climate.

Fair Weather Fact

At any given time, on average there are about 1,800 thunderstorms occurring on Earth with 100 lightning strikes per second.

Well Said...

What dreadful hot weather we have! It keeps me in a continual state of inelegance.

Jane Austen

World's Worst 20th-century Weather Disasters

Hurricanes/cyclones

Tropical cyclones that develop in the tropics or sub-tropics are characterised by low pressure, wind speeds in excess of 75mph (120km/h), extensive precipitation and bands of cumulonimbus clouds that spiral in towards a central eye. In the Western Hemisphere such events are called hurricanes, but in the East they are known as cyclones or typhoons.

As you can see from the list below, the Indian sub-continent is especially vulnerable to such devastating cyclones. The resulting high fatalities are due to the densely populated, low lying land but the final death toll is always exacerbated by diseases spread by infected water and crop failure.

Date	Location	Approx. no. of Deaths	Name of cyclone
November 1970	Bangladesh (East Pakistan)	500,000	Bhola
April 1991	Bangladesh	140,000	Cyclone 02B
May 2008	Burma (Myanmar)	100,000	Cyclone Nargis
August 1975	China	100,000	Typhoon Nina
May 1965 (two cyclones)	Bangladesh (East Pakistan)	42,000	Bengal Cyclone
October 1942	China	40,000	Andhra
November 1977	India	20,000	Pradesh Cyclone
October–November 1998	Central America	11,000–18,000	Hurricane Mitch
September 1971	India	10,000	Orissa Cyclone
October 1999	India	10,000	Cyclone 05B

Floods

Historically, floods have been the deadliest of all natural disasters. Traditionally, rivers have provided fertile land for agriculture, a ready supply of water and a means of communication, and consequently these areas have become highly populated. However, river plains are, by their nature, low-lying areas prone to flooding, either following periods of high rainfall (such as the monsoon season), the destruction of dams – either during war or as a result of tropical storms, or by the process of silting, which in particular affects the Yellow River and others in China. Please note the estimated number of deaths given here includes those affected by outbreaks of disease that often follow severe floods as well as famine created by the destruction of crops and livestock.

Date	Location	Approx. no. of Deaths
1931	Yellow River, China	1–3 million
1939	Yellow River, China	500,000–900,000
1975	Banqioa Dam, China (Typhoon Nina)	231,000
2004	Indonesia (tsunami)	230,000
1935	Yangtze River, China	145,000
1971	Haoi, Red River Delta, North Vietnam	100,000
1911	Yangtze River, China	100,000
1999	Venezuela	10,000
1951	Manchuria	4,800
1998	Bangladesh	1,000

Global Warming:
How You Can Help...

Environmentalism is the political hot potato of the last 20 years. It is the most pressing issue the planet is facing before we reach what scientists refer to as 'The Point Of No Return': the point at which the damage done to Earth's ecosystems and atmosphere – due to CO_2 emissions – becomes irreversible. Inevitably this will continue to seriously affect the weather.

Of course, it doesn't have to be that way. You can help. Here are the Top 10 things you can do to help cut down on your carbon footprint at home:

1. Replace your light bulbs with compact fluorescent light bulbs. These use 60% less energy than a regular bulb. This one change alone could save about 300lbs in CO_2 emissions each year, per home.
2. Turn off your appliances properly. Don't just leave things on standby. A TV set that's left on standby mode uses 40% more energy.
3. Get double glazing. It's estimated you can save more than 70% of the energy lost through single-glazed windows.
4. When cooking on the hob, cover your pans.
5. Use the washing machine at a lower temperature setting. Cleaning detergents are now just as effective on lower temperatures. Also, always clean a full load and never just a few items.
6. Take a shower. Baths use up to four times more energy. Use a low-flow showerhead too if you can and limit the time you spend in the shower to five minutes.
7. Use a clothesline instead of a tumble dryer. Tumble dryers are one of the worst appliances for energy consumption.

8. Recycle. Up to 60% of all paper and plastic products are able to be recycled. Check the packaging and recycle accurately with council-supplied recycling bags. Buy products that only use minimal packaging.
9. Reuse your plastic shopping bags when going to the supermarket instead of using new ones each time.
10. Switch to green power. Go online and check out alternative electricity company websites such as www.ecotricity.co.uk that offer green power at affordable prices.

Morning Hymn

Morning has broken, like the first morning
Blackbird has spoken, like the first bird
Praise for the singing, praise for the morning
Praise for the springing fresh from the word

Sweet the rain's new fall, sunlit from heaven
Like the first dewfall, on the first grass
Praise for the sweetness of the wet garden
Sprung in completeness where his feet pass

Mine is the sunlight, mine is the morning
Born of the one light, Eden saw play
Praise with elation, praise every morning
God's recreation of the new day

Words by Eleanor Farjeon, 1931

International Weather Symbols: Drizzle

Light intermittent   ,

Light continuous   ,,

Moderate intermittent   ;

Moderate continuous   , ,

Heavy intermittent   ;

Heavy continuous   ,;,

When to Visit ... St Petersburg

June
Av. daily sunshine: 10 hrs
Av. monthly rainfall: 2in (50mm)
Av. max. temperature: 20°C (68°F)

Extreme Weather Heroes

- **Icarus** (The boy who flew too close to the sun)
- **Ernest Shackleton** (his *Endurance* was tested by Antartica)
- **Steve Fossett** (the man who flew around the world in a balloon)
- **Nando Perrado** (one of the survivors of Uruguayan Air Force Flight 571 which crash landed in the Andes mountains in 1972)

🐾 🐾 🐾

Halcyon Days

The halcyon is a mythical fabulous bird, often identified as a kingfisher, that made its nest floating directly on the sea. In order to give its eggs time to hatch, it cast a spell to calm the waves. The charm lasted for one week before and one week after the Winter Solstice, after which the storms closed in. These were the halcyon days – a time of year when the Mediterranean is indeed generally calm. The term is often used loosely to refer to any peaceful or happy time, but which more precisely means the calm before the storm.

In classical mythology, Alcyone was the daughter of Aeolus, the god of the wind. When her husband was killed in a storm, she threw herself into the sea, at which the gods turned them both into kingfishers. Her name survives in the Latin names of various species of kingfisher (such as Halcyon smyrnensis (White-throated Kingfisher) and Ceryle alcyon (Belted Kingfisher)).

Weather Playlist Part II: Newies

'It's Raining Men' – The Weather Girls
'Weather Storm' – Massive Attack
'After the Storm' – Mumford and Sons
'Black Rain' – Ozzy Osbourne
'Blinded by Rainbows' – The Rolling Stones
'Butterflies And Hurricanes' – Muse
'Crying Lightning' – Arctic Monkeys
'Don't Let the Sun Go Down on Me' – Elton John
'Electrical Storm' – U2
'No Rain' – Blind Melon
'This is a Low' – Blur
'Lightning Crashes' – Live
'Weather With You' – Crowded House

The Poet in Autumn

O Autumn, laden with fruit, and stained
With the blood of the grape, pass not, but sit
Beneath my shady roof; there thou mayest rest
And tune thy jolly voice to my fresh pipe,
And all the daughters of the year shall dance!
Sing now the lusty song of fruits and flowers.

William Blake, 'To Autumn'

Airline Strikes

Flying through thunderclouds – as they inevitably do from time to time – aircraft may actually trigger lightning by providing a highly conductive path for it. The average commercial airliner can expect this to happen about once a year, in fact. The bolt often passes through the length of the plane, usually harmlessly.

Aircraft parts are actually tested and certified for airworthiness with the possibility of lightning strike in mind. In the UK, there is a dedicated artificial lightning testing rig at the village of Culham in Oxfordshire, where nosecones and 'radomes' (radar domes) are put through their paces. Thus the damage caused by a lightning strike is usually minor. As long as the structure stays intact and controllable, and the fuel tanks are safe, there is no danger; the passengers are inside a perfect Faraday cage.

There is, however, always a worst-case scenario. On 8 December 1963, tragedy struck Pan American Flight 214 from San Juan in Puerto Rico to Philadelphia International. The left wing of a four-engine Boeing 707-121 was hit by lightning and a fuel tank ignited; it exploded and crashed at Elkton, Maryland with the loss of all 81 lives. The pilot hardly had time to issue a mayday call. To the accident investigators, the melted rivets of the wing told a clear story and, as a result, lightning discharge wicks were immediately made compulsory. Onboard electronics are electromagnetically shielded (thanks again, Franklin and Faraday). You'll be fine.

Monet-ing About the Weather

For me, a landscape does not exist in its own right, since its appearance changes at every moment; but the surrounding atmosphere brings it to life – the light and the air which vary continually. For me, it is only the surrounding atmosphere which gives subjects their true value.

Claude Monet, artist

Fair Weather Fact

The average lifespan of a tornado is less than 15 minutes.

A Joke For All Seasons

If a band plays music in a thunderstorm, who is most likely to get hit by lightning?
The conductor.

Lines of Latitude

Sailors can usually be relied upon for a colourful term to leaven the ubiquitous Latin of scientific discourse, and they have done us proud with their terms for lines of latitude.

Just to recap, for those whose attention was distracted in the back row of the geography class by the graffiti on the desk in front of them, we have latitude and longitude, respectively the horizontal lines and the vertical ones if you look at the world in its notional north–south vertical orientation, as seen in spinning globes and novelty drinks cabinets, with Australia at the bottom. The zero line of longitude or Prime Meridian, as internationally accepted today, passes – how convenient! – through the Royal Observatory at Greenwich. It is marked by a metal strip in the courtyard for the tourists to straddle, and nowadays also by a green laser shining out proudly from the wall of the building, somewhat less conveniently placed for novelty snapshot opportunities. The North Pole is 90° north and the South Pole is 90° south, with the Equator at 0° of latitude. The Arctic Circle is found at some 66° (and, to be accurate, 33 minutes and 39 seconds) north, with the Antarctic Circle at the same latitude south. So far, so not very colourful.

The Tropics of Cancer and Capricorn (leaving aside the raunchy novels of those names written by Henry Miller in the 1930s) represent the extremes of the sun's path across the sky at different seasons. They are the most northerly and southerly latitudes at which the sun can appear directly overhead at noon at the summer and winter equinoxes, in other words, when the relevant hemisphere is maximally tilted towards the sun. However, for reasons that need not concern us here, this location changes over time, so that, unlike the Arctic and Antarctic Circles and the Equator, these lines actually move across the globe. At the moment, they lie at 23° 26 minutes 21 seconds North and South respectively, but when these names were invented some 2,000 years ago, the sun was aligned with the constellations of Cancer (the crab) and Capricorn (the goat). Nowadays, they would be the tropics of Gemini and Taurus. But any of these names is surely more stylish than calling them the Northern and Southern Tropic.

Sailors, of course, are much preoccupied with prevailing winds. Between 40°S and 50°S, with no significant landmass to slow them down, they are distinctly boisterous, and this region is traditionally known as the Roaring Forties – not to be confused with the Roaring Twenties which refers to the decade of that name, with its fast cars, fast women and terrifyingly decadent jazz music. Thus we have the Furious Fifties (50°S to 60°S) and the Shrieking, or Screaming, Sixties (60°S and below). Of course, by the time you get to 70°S, there's very little sea left between you and the South Pole, so sailors never needed to invent wind-based names for those latitudes, and they had probably used up all the best alliterative adjectives anyway.

Record Weather: Highest/Lowest Pressure

An air pressure of 1083.8mb was recorded at Agata in Siberia on 31 December 1968. During Typhoon Tip in the Pacific Ocean west of Guam on 12 October 1979, the pressure dropped to 870mb.

When to Visit ... Barbados

February
Av. daily sunshine: 9 hrs
Av. monthly rainfall: 1in (28mm)
Av. max. temperature: 28°C (82.4°F)

A Joke For All Seasons

Where in a jail should you put a tornado?
In a high pressure cell.

The Poet in Winter

The English winter – ending in July,
To recommence in August.

Lord Byron, 'Don Juan'

WINTER

Fossil Lightning

How do you keep a wave that breaks on the sand? How do you hold a moonbeam in your hand? Well, scientists are still working on that one, but it is almost possible to hold a bolt of lightning in your hand – in the form of sand. A bolt of lightning can travel at 100,000mph (160,934km/h), carrying many millions of volts. At about 28,000°C (50,432°F), several times hotter than the surface of the sun, it is easily hot enough to melt sand into glass.

And this is exactly what can happen when a bolt of lightning hits, say, a beach or a sand dune. It leaves a little tube of glass in the sand, usually just a few inches long. The correct term for this object is a fulgurite. In layman's terms, the result can look like anything from a fossilised dog turd to a piece of twisted lead piping. The outside is usually rough and knobbly where the energy has branched out just like a lightning bolt in the sky, and naturally has a sandy texture, but the interior has a glossy lining made of natural glass called lechatelierite (amorphous silicon dioxide).

Artificial fulgurites have been successfully produced by simply passing a high-voltage current through a pile of sand. One even happened naturally in a pile of sand at a builder's merchants. In an empty desert with no projecting objects to help lightning find its way to earth, the formation of a fulgurite must be a common enough occurrence, though the little piece of glass is unlikely to survive and be found by anyone. But every now and again, it will be captured and fossilised by the normal geological processes that turn a stretch of sand into sandstone. A famous example was found in 1966 on a beach near the village of Corrie on the isle of Arran off the west coast of Scotland. It had been formed some 250 million years ago by a lightning strike over what were then desert sands.

Well Said...

Conversation about the weather is the last refuge of the unimaginative.

Oscar Wilde, writer, poet and playwright

❈ ❈ ❈

Top 10 Worst Effects of Global Warming

1. Destruction of ecosystems: global warming and the increase in carbon emissions are affecting physical and biological systems on land and in the sea.
2. Loss of biodiversity: increasing numbers of species are becoming endangered or are being lost through global warming.
3. Conflicts and war: drought can further exacerbate conflict in particular areas as opposing factions compete for water supplies and land capable of sustaining agriculture.
4. Economic consequences: weather-related disasters cause huge amounts of damage and can cause disease.
5. Disease: the increase in floods and droughts appears to be causing an increase in diseases spread by species such as mosquitoes, ticks and mice.
6. Drought: drought conditions are set to increase dramatically in certain areas, causing a decrease in drinking water and deterioration in agricultural output.

7. Storms and floods: severe storms are becoming increasingly frequent.
8. Heat waves: record temperatures are becoming more common; the European heat wave in 2003 killed an estimated 35,000 people.
9. Shrinking glaciers: rising temperatures are causing glaciers to retreat and permafrost to melt.
10. Rising sea level: as temperatures rise it is estimated that melting icecaps could cause sea levels to rise by 20ft (6m) by 2100.

❋ ❋ ❋

Useful Metaphors: Relationships

She unloaded a *hail* of abuse at him!
They are getting married after a *whirlwind* romance!
He gave me an *icy* stare.
She always has such a *sunny* disposition.

❋ ❋ ❋

When to Visit ... Beijing

May
Av. daily sunshine: 9 hrs
Av. monthly rainfall: 1¼in (35mm)
Av. max. temperature: 27°C (80.6°F)

Seasonal Recipes
Winter Hotpot

Preparation Time 20 minutes, plus marinating · Cooking Time 2 hours 20 minutes · Serves: 8 · Per Serving 580 calories, 28g fat (of which 10g saturates), 31g carbohydrate

3lb (1.4kg) boned shoulder of pork, cut into 1in (2.5cm) cubes
6 garlic cloves, crushed
7 tbsp olive oil
2 tbsp red wine vinegar
4 tbsp soft brown sugar
2 tsp minced chilli or a few drops of chilli sauce
3 tsp dried oregano
2 tsp dried thyme
1lb (450g) onions, peeled, halved and sliced
2 tbsp tomato purée
2 × 400g cans haricot or flageolet beans, drained and juice put to one side
2 × 400g cans chopped tomatoes
10fl oz (300ml) red wine
4 bay leaves
1oz (25g) butter
4oz (125g) white breadcrumbs from French bread or ciabatta
4oz (125g) grated Gruyère cheese
Fresh thyme sprigs to garnish

1   Put the pork in a large bowl with the garlic, 2 tbsp oil, the vinegar, sugar, chilli, salt, pepper, 2 tsp oregano and all the thyme. Combine all the ingredients, cover and leave in the fridge for at least 8 hours to marinate.

2   Drain the pork, putting the marinade to one side.

3   Preheat the oven to 180°C (160°C fan oven), gas mark 4.
    Heat 3 tbsp oil in a large flameproof casserole and fry the
    pork in batches until well browned and sealed on all sides.
    Put to one side. Add the remaining oil with the onions
    and cook for 10 minutes over a high heat, stirring
    occasionally, until they are soft and caramelised. Add the
    tomato purée and cook for one minute. Put the meat back
    into the casserole with the drained bean juice, tomatoes,
    wine, bay leaves and the reserved marinade. Bring to the
    boil, stirring, then cover and cook in the oven for two
    hours or until the pork is very tender.

4   About 20 minutes before the end of the cooking time, stir
    in the beans.

5   Increase the oven temperature to 200°C (180°C fan
    oven), gas mark 6 and move the pork to a lower shelf. Heat
    the butter in a roasting tin; add the breadcrumbs, the
    remaining oregano and seasoning. Brown on the top shelf
    for 10 minutes. Sprinkle the hotpot with the breadcrumbs
    and grated cheese. Garnish with thyme sprigs and serve.

❊   ❊   ❊

The Clerk of the Weather

Clerk of the Weather (Office): an imaginary functionary humorously supposed to control the state of the weather.
Oxford English Dictionary

A quaint expression, certainly, and one which amused the American novelist Nathaniel Hawthorne (1804–1864) enough to give him the idea for a short story, 'A Visit to the Clerk of the Weather' (1836).

'I don't know – I have not yet spoken to the clerk of the weather,' – said I, in common parlance to my friend and kinsman, who had asked me the wise question – 'Do you think we shall have an early spring?'

A little old woman in a grey cloak appears and whisks the narrator away through the clouds to another planet where he actually meets the Clerk of the Weather himself, along with his assistants Jack Frost and Spring, in a huge cave whether the weather comes from.

'There were three gigantic beings lounging about in different parts of the room, while a venerable, stately old man, with long gray locks, sat at the farther side of the apartment busily engaged in writing. Before advancing to speak to any of my new acquaintances, I glanced around the rocky cavern. In one corner was piled a heap of red-hot thunderbolts. Against the wall hung several second-hand rainbows, covered with dust and much faded. Several hundred cart loads of hail-stones, two large sacks of wind, and a portable tempest, firmly secured with iron bands, next engaged my attention ... I sauntered about the cavern to examine its singular contents. A gigantic fellow was sweating over the fire and cooking his master's breakfast. In a moment, I saw him ascend by a sort of rope ladder, and pick a small white cloud out of the heavens wherewith to settle the coffee. I sauntered on until I came to a heap of granite, behind which sat a dozen little black fellows, cross-legged, who were laboring with all their might to weave a thunder gust. The part of the business which seemed to puzzle them most was, the working in of the bolts, which they were obliged to handle with long pincers.'

The Poet in Winter

There's a certain slant of light,
On winter afternoons,
That oppresses, like the weight
Of Cathedral tunes.

Emily Dickinson, 'There's a Certain Slant of Light'

❊　❊　❊

Under the Weather: Part III
(Weather clichés as pure as driven snow)

- On cloud nine
- Three sheets to the wind
- Throwing caution to the wind
- The tides beginning to turn
- Walking on sunshine
- Fair weather friends
- Weather the storm
- When it rains it pours
- Still waters run deep

❋ ❋ ❋

Well Said...

The best thing one can do when it's raining is to let it rain.

Henry Wadsworth Longfellow, poet and educator

❋ ❋ ❋

A Devilish Definition

In his *Devil's Dictionary*, American writer Ambrose Bierce (1842–1914) included the following entries:

WEATHER (noun)
The climate of the hour. A permanent topic of conversation among persons whom it does not interest, but who have inherited the tendency to chatter about it from naked arboreal ancestors whom it keenly concerned. The setting up of official weather bureaus and their maintenance in mendacity prove that even governments are accessible to suasion by the rude forefathers of the jungle.

Once I dipt into the future far as human eye could see,
And I saw the Chief Forecaster, dead as any one can be –
Dead and damned and shut in Hades as a liar from his birth,
With a record of unreason seldom paralleled on earth.
While I looked he reared him solemnly, that incandescent youth,
From the coals that he'd preferred to the advantages of truth.
He cast his eyes about him and above him; then he wrote
On a slab of thin asbestos what I venture here to quote –
For I read it in the rose-light of the everlasting glow:
'Cloudy; variable winds, with local showers; cooler; snow.'

Halcyon Jones

❋ ❋ ❋

Weather Birds

Birds are closely linked with the weather. Being creatures of the air, they can hardly escape it. They even help us predict it. Swallows fly low when bad weather is on the way, because the insects they feed on are forced downwards in low pressure. Some people are convinced ducks swim round and round in circles in freezing weather in order to prevent the water from icing up.

Sure enough, many birds have common names to do with the weather. The storm petrel or stormy petrel is a family of seabirds (Hydrobatidae) which were thought to herald a storm. The other part of their name supposedly comes from their distinctive way of half-flying, half-walking across the water. Petrel is said to be a reference to Saint Peter, who walked on the water – or at least, he tried to, as we read in Matthew 14:28–31: 'But when he saw the wind boisterous, he was afraid; and beginning to sink, he cried, saying, Lord, save me. And immediately Jesus stretched forth his hand, and caught him, and said unto him, O thou of little faith, wherefore didst thou doubt?'

An equally poetic image is conjured up by the old folk name for the kestrel (Falco tinnunculus), 'windhover', immortalised in Gerard Manley Hopkins's poem of the same name ('I caught this morning morning's minion...'). Another name for the kestrel, allegedly, is 'fleingall', which some would have us believe means 'fly-in-gale'; however, we must come clean here and note that more respectable authorities cast doubt on this interpretation, considering it no more than a misprint deriving from a supposed German word Steingall, itself of (as the *Oxford English Dictionary* sniffily remarks) 'doubtful genuineness'. Sixteenth-century sources claimed this steingall to be in fact an English word, which we find elsewhere as standgall, imaginatively parsed as 'stand-in-gale'. This more usual form staniel derives from an Anglo-Saxon word meaning literally 'stone-yeller', a poetic reference to the bird's cry. And from there it comes to be used as an insult – a transition that would be lost on us today, but which in the age of falconry alluded to the fact that the kestrel was the least valued of all birds of prey: 'an Eagle for an Emperor ... a Peregrine for a Prince ... and a kestrel for a knave'.

The wind thrush is a local name for the redwing (Turdus iliacus), and the winter crow is better known as the hooded crow (Corvus cornix). The term rain-bird or rain-fowl has been applied to a wide range of species, but in Britain most often refers to the green woodpecker, which answers to a long list of quaint folk names including rain-pie and weather cock, and whose call is supposed to be a sign of rain. Other rain-birds include the red-throated diver, also known in Shetland as the rain goose; the mistle-thrush; and, perhaps most exotically, Psophodes nigrogularis, the so-called western whipbird or black-throated coachwhip-bird.

❋　❋　❋

The Poet in Winter

Old Winter, with his frosty beard,
Thus once to Jove his prayer preferred:
'What have I done of all the year,
To bear this hated doom severe?
My cheerless suns no pleasure know;
Night's horrid car drags, dreary slow;
My dismal months no joys are crowning,
But spleeny English hanging, drowning.

Robert Burns, 'Impromptu On Mrs. Riddell's Birthday'

❈ ❈ ❈

Nephelococcygia

Nephelococcygia: the term applied when people find familiar objects within the shape of a cloud.

❉ ❉ ❉

Snow Blink

Moving across the seemingly interminable wastes of the Arctic or Antarctic, how can you see what lies ahead? Indigenous people and explorers know to look up at the sky. Just as you can see the night lights of a city illuminating the clouds above it, the clouds can act as a kind of faint mirror of the terrain below them – what's rather poetically known as the 'sky map'. Snow blink is not, as you might have guessed, the after-effect of not wearing your tinted goggles, but the white glare on the underside of the cloud base that tells you you're moving towards a snow-covered area, as opposed to ice, which casts a slightly less bright glow on to the clouds, known as ice blink. 'Land sky' is a darker glow and 'water sky' darker still, often showing up as darker streaks projected on to the clouds, a beacon for mariners aiming to avoid their ship getting trapped in the ice.

❉ ❉ ❉

Winter Words

When winter first begins to bite and stones crack in the frosty night, when pools are black and trees are bare, 'tis evil in the Wild to fare.

JRR Tolkein, *The Fellowship of the Ring*

❄ ❄ ❄

Fair Weather Fact

For each minute of the day, 1 billion tons of rain fall on Earth.

❄ ❄ ❄

Well Said...

Everybody talks about the weather,
but nobody does anything about it.

Mark Twain

❄ ❄ ❄

Act of God?

Christians in America do like to make a statement. When Lawrence and Darlene Bishop founded the Solid Rock church near Munroe, Ohio, they thought big. They spent about $250,000 building a 62ft(18m) statue of Jesus Christ out of polystyrene and fibreglass. Entitled 'King of Kings', the statue was constructed on an island in a huge baptismal pool; arms raised heavenwards as if to bless the trucks thundering by on nearby Interstate 75, it reminded some of a referee signalling a touchdown in a game of American football. Coloured spotlights and water jets in the pool completed what must have been a truly startling effect; 'it sort of looms out at you, especially at night,' said a trucker.

Or rather, it did. Sometime in the stormy night of 14 June 2010, an even more impressive effect was achieved when the statue was struck by lightning and went up like a torch. Touchdown Jesus had turned into a kind of high-tech Wicker Man. Flames soared 30ft (9m) above its outstretched hands; a huge tailback of rubberneckers formed on the Interstate, and in the morning only the blackened steel frame was left.

The church plans to rebuild the statue, which it seems was insured for half a million dollars. The only thing is, will they be able to bring themselves to claim it on the form as an 'Act of God'?

❋ ❋ ❋

Snowy Words

Our English word snow comes straight from Anglo-Saxon, snáw. Indeed, that is the form that has survived to this day in Scots, where someone or something can be said to vanish 'like snaw aff a dyke (stone wall)'.

There is also a nautical term snow, or snaw, defined in the *Oxford English Dictionary* as 'a small sailing-vessel resembling a brig, carrying a main and fore mast and a supplementary trysail mast close behind the mainmast; formerly employed as a warship', but that comes from Dutch and is not connected with the weather.

English, being a sort of magpie language that collects bits and pieces from all over the globe, usually has a dozen different words for everything; but in this case we seem to have gone no further than Latin. However, the language of Ancient Rome (nix, nivis, third declension, feminine, 'snow') has done us proud for snowy synonyms. In technical parlance, a nival region is one that has received considerable nivation (snowfall) and, thus nivated (besnowed, in English), is naturally characterised by its nivosity. Poetically speaking, it would tend to demonstrate a ninguid or niveous quality. Nivôse was the name of the fourth month of the French Republican calendar introduced in 1793, which ran from 21 December to 19 January.

Casting around for non-Latin niveousness, we might mention the splendid harfang or harphang, another name for the snowy owl (Bubo scandiacus). It comes to us from Swedish, where it literally means a hare-catcher. And we really cannot close without paying tribute to one word from Old English: 'flother', a snowflake – the kind of word that dictionaries mark 'rare' and 'obscure', but one which surely deserves wider currency.

The Cloud Spotter's Bride

— *Ma petite folle bien-aimée me donnait à dîner, et par la fenêtre ouverte de
la salle à manger je contemplais les mouvantes architectures que Dieu fait avec
les vapeurs, les merveilleuses constructions de l'impalpable. Et je me disais, à
travers ma contemplation: 'Toutes ces fantasmagories sont presque aussi belles
que les yeux de ma belle bien-aimée, la petite folle monstrueuse aux yeux verts'.*
— *Et tout-à-coup je reçus un violent coup de poing dans le dos, et j'entendis une
vois rauque et charmante, une voix histérique et comme enrouée par l'eau-de-
vie, la voix de ma chère petite bien-aimée, qui me disait, 'Allez-vous bientôt
manger votre soupe, sacré bougre de marchand de nuages?'*

 – My dear little idiot was giving me dinner, and through the
open window of the dining-room I was gazing at the moving
architecture God makes out of vapour, those wondrous
constructions of intangibility. And I thought to myself as I
gazed: 'All these phantasmagorias are almost as beautiful as
the eyes of my fair beloved, my little mad monster with the
green eyes'.
– And suddenly I got a heavy thump in the back and I heard
a harsh, charming voice, as if hoarse with brandy, the voice of
my dear little beloved, saying 'are you going to eat your soup
now or what, you god-damn cloud-merchant?'

Charles Baudelaire, *'La Soupe et les Nuages'*

※　※　※

The Poet in Winter

When icicles hang by the wall
And Dick the shepherd blows his nail,
And Tom bears logs into the hall,
And milk comes frozen home in pail;
When blood is nipt, and ways be foul,
Then nightly sings the staring owl
Tu-whoo!
To-whit, Tu-whoo! A merry note!
While greasy Joan doth keel the pot.

William Shakespeare, Love's Labour's Lost

❄ ❄ ❄

Fair Weather Fact

The largest hailstone ever recorded in the United States was nearly the size of a (British) football – it measured 7in (18cm) in diameter.

❊   ❊   ❊

A New Type of Cloud?

The system of cloud classification in use today was devised by Luke Howard, refined by others and eventually enshrined by the World Meteorological Organization in its *International Cloud Atlas*, first published in 1896. No new type of cloud has been admitted to this hallowed pantheon since 1951.

However, in 2009, a whippersnapper of an amateur cloud-fancier proposed a brand-new 'species'. Gavin Pretor-Pinney, for it is he, suggests the name asperatus ('roughened'), to suggest a texture like a wind-blown sea. To others it might perhaps suggest the surface of a bowl of thick whipping-cream roughly stirred with a wooden spoon – in the highly hypothetical situation where the giant mixing-bowl were lifted and held upside-down above our heads. As proposed, it's a species of the Undulatus genus, though research suggests it may be related to the recognised mammatus ('pouched') texture most often associated with cumulonimbus but also found on stratocumulus, altocumulus, altostratus or cirrus clouds.

So, two centuries after the dawn of scientific cloud study, how has this one managed to escape official notice for so long? Well, it's not something you see every day, in fact, it's downright rare: 'the Yeti of clouds' according to its champion, who became aware of it when American cloud spotters sent in dramatic photos from such places as Iowa and Texas (it seems to be found especially in the Plains states of the United States, after the passage of thunderstorms). And try as we might to be systematic, the naming of clouds will probably always have some suggestive element to it, in terms of distinguishing shapes in the sky and ascribing them to classifications. We can only wait to see what the sages of the IMO have to say on the matter.

❊ ❊ ❊

A Joke For All Seasons

Why do mother kangaroos hate rainy days?
Because then the children have to play inside.

❊ ❊ ❊

Top 10 Species in Danger from Global Warming

1. Clownfish
2. Emperor penguin
3. Koala bear
4. Beluga whale
5. Leatherback turtle
6. Quiver tree
7. Staghorn coral
8. Arctic fox
9. Ringed sea
10. Salmon

※ ※ ※

The Poet in Winter

O Winter! ruler of the inverted year, …
I crown thee king of intimate delights,
Fireside enjoyments, home-born happiness,
And all the comforts that the lowly roof
Of undisturb'd Retirement, and the hours
Of long uninterrupted evening, know.

William Cowper, 'Task'

※ ※ ※

Coup de Poudre

We might think of lightning strikes as an individual hazard, but a single strike can kill dozens in the right circumstances. It is not uncommon for an entire herd of cattle to be killed while sheltering under a tree during a thunderstorm. In August 1769, lightning killed, directly or indirectly, some 3,000 people in Brescia, Italy, when the Church of San Nazaro was struck. Unfortunately, its vaults housed around 90 tons of gunpowder. The fire that ensued destroyed one sixth of the city. Remember – never keep your explosive stockpiles in a tall building, even if it has a useful basement.

❈ ❈ ❈

Well Said...

Winter is nature's way of saying, 'Up yours.'

Robert Byrne, author and billiards champion

❈ ❈ ❈

A Joke For All Seasons

It only rains twice a year in Britain: August to April and May to July...

Weather Cocktails: Part IV

Springtime   Pineapple juice, peach-flavoured.

White Snow   Galliano, passion-fruit juice, light
                        cream, white crème de cacao, ground
                        cinnamon, star fruit.

Apple Sunset   Calvados, crème de cassis, grenadine,
                        orange juice, 1 maraschino cherry.

Moonlight Cup   Apple juice, Calvados, sugar, ginger ale,
                        1 slice of lemon.

Summer in Italy   Amaro Siciliano, gin, 1 orange segment,
                        tonic water.

Red Lightning   Amaro Siciliano, Campari, soda water, 1
                        lemon peel spiral, maraschino cherry.

Tornado   Grapefruit juice, passion-fruit juice,
                        tequila, peach-flavoured liquer, lime
                        cordial, half slice of orange, 2
                        maraschino cherries.

London Fog   Annisett, white peppermint-flavoured
Cocktail   liquer, Angostura bitters, sprig of mint.

❋ ❋ ❋

Fair Weather Fact

The total amount of precipitation to fall to Earth in one year is 5,000 billion tons.

❁ ❁ ❁

Well Said...

Spring is nature's way of saying, 'Let's party!'

Robin Williams

❁ ❁ ❁

Old Cow's Tale

A cow with its tail to the West makes the weather best,
A cow with its tail to the East makes the weather least.

❁ ❁ ❁

The Path to Earth

Prior to the invention of the lightning conductor in the mid-18th century, the bell tower of St Mark's Basilica in Venice was damaged by lightning nine times between 1338 and 1762. In 1766, a lightning conductor was installed and no further damage from lightning has occurred since.

The first English lightning conductor was installed at the Eddystone Lighthouse in 1760. After initial scepticism, the court of King George III decided to adopt recommendations concerning lightning conduction made by Benjamin Franklin, and by 1772 lightning conductors had been installed at, among other prominent landmarks, Buckingham Palace, St Paul's, St James's Church and Blenheim Palace.

The introduction of the lightning conductor certainly had happier results than the old belief that thunder could be warded off by the ringing of church bells – a dangerous occupation, to put it mildly, during an electrical storm with a wet rope connecting you to the tallest structure for miles around.

❋   ❋   ❋

A Joke For All Seasons

Who is it that everybody listens to but nobody believes? The weatherman.

Further Reading

General Weather titles

Atmosphere, Weather and Climate, Roger G. Barry (Routledge, 2009)

Weather for Dummies, John D. Cox (John Wiley & Sons, 2000)

The Weather Book: Why it Happens and Where it Comes From, Diana Craig (Michael O'Mara Books Ltd, 2009)

Oxford Dictionary of Weather, Storm Dunlop (Oxford University Press, 2008)

Great British Weather Disasters, Philip Eden (Continuum, 2008)

Cloud Book: How to Understand the Skies, Richard Hamblyn (David & Charles, 2008)

The MET Office Book of the British Weather, The Met Office (David & Charles, 2010)

The Cloudspotter's Guide, Gavin Pretor-Pinney (Sceptre, 2007)

The Royal Meteorological Society Weather Watcher's 3-year Log Book (Frances Lincoln, 2007)

Since Records Began ... The Highs and Lows of Britain's Weather, Paul Simons (Collins, 2008)

The Weather Handbook, Alan Watts (Adlard Coles Nautical, 2004)

Climate Change titles

Want to read up on the topical issue of climate change? Here is a selected bibliography to get you started:

The Weather Makers: Our Changing Climate and What it Means For Life on Earth, Tim Flannery (Penguin, 2007)

The Economics and Politics of Climate Change, Dieter Helm (Oxford, 2009)

Why We Disagree About Climate Change: Understanding Controversy, Inaction and Opportunity, Mike Hulme (Cambridge University Press, 2009)

The Hot Topic: How to Tackle Global Warming and Still Keep the Lights On, David King (Bloomsbury Publishing, 2009)

Fixing Climate: The Story of Climate Science — and How to Stop Global Warming, Robert Kunzig & Wallace S. Broecker (Green Profile, 2009)

An Appeal to Reason: A Cool Look at Global Warming, Nigel Lawson (Gerald Duckworth & Co Ltd, 2009)

The Science and Politics of Global Climate Change: A Guide to the Debate, Andrew Dessler & Edward A. Parson (Cambridge University Press, 2010)

Climate Confusion, Roy W. Spencer (Encounter Books, 2010)

Sources

2   Fair Weather Fact, www.funshun.com/amazing-facts;

7   When to Visit ... Data taken from *Weather to Travel*,
        Tomorrow's Guides Ltd (1998), Fair Weather Fact,
        Guinness World Records;

8   Not-very-musical Instruments, www.ehow.com;

12   When to Visit...as p.7;

20   St Swithin's Day
        www.guardian.co.uk/uk/2010/jul/15/st
        swithins-day-wet/print;

24   When to Visit ... as p.7;

25   Seven Things You Never Wanted to Know About
        Global
        Warming,http://news.nationalgeographic.com/news
        /2004/12/1206_041206_global_warming.html;

26   Seasonal Recipes, *Good Housekeeping Favourite Comfort Food*;

29   When to Visit ... as p.7;

31   Fair Weather Fact, as p.2; 38 The Rain Man,
        www.guardian.co.uk/uk/2010/jul/15/st-swithins
        daywet/print;

45   When to Visit ... as p.7;

49   Top 10 British Weather Disasters: Part I,
        www.metoffice.gov.uk, www.bbc.co.uk/weather; 50
        Under the Weather: Part I, www.gardendigest.com;

53   Fair Weather Fact, as p.2;

54   When to Visit ... as p.7;

58   When to Visit ... as p.7;

59   Seasonal Recipes, *Good Housekeeping Cookbook*;

61   Top 10 Beaches, Yahoo! Travel;

70   When to Visit ... as p.7;

74   When to Visit ... as p.7;

81   When to Visit ... as p.7; Fair Weather Fact, as p.2,
When to Visit ... as p.7;

84   The Great Storm: Part II, www.bbc.co.uk/weather;

89   When to Visit ... as p.7;

92   Under the Weather: Part II, as p.49;

98   In Case of an Emergency ... *Good Housekeeping Ultimate Book of the Home* (2010); 100 When to Visit ... as p.7;

101   Top 10 British Weather Disasters: Part II, as p.48;

106   Seasonal Recipes, *Good Housekeeping Favourite Comfort Food*;

108   When to Visit ... as p.7;

110   Lost in Translation, www.20000-names.com;

112   Fair Weather Fact, as p.2;

113   When to Visit ... as p.7;

122   Fair Weather Fact, as p.2;

122   World's Worst 20th-century Weather Disasters, www.epicdisasters.com, www.wunderground.com;

124   Global Warming: How You Can Help, http://globalwarming-facts.info/50-tips.html;

126   When to Visit ... as p.7;

130   Fair Weather Fact, as p.2;

133   When to Visit ... as p.7;

136   Top 10 Worst Effects of Global Warming, science.howstuffworks.com/worst-effects-global-warming6.htm;

137   When to Visit ... as p.7;

138   Seasonal Recipes, *Good Housekeeping Family Cookbook*;

142   Under the Weather: Part III, as p.49;

155   Top 10 Species in Danger from Global Warming, www.telegraph.co.uk;

156   Fair Weather Fact, as p.2

Answers

Not-very-Musical-Instruments (from p.8)

1. d.
2. h.
3. f.
4. g.
5. a.
6. c.
7. i.
8. e.

Acknowledgments

For my dear mother,

Thanks to Malcolm at Portico, whose patience is as sunny as the day is long, and to Katie Hewett, Katie Cowan and Zoe Anspach.

My old friend Prof. Giles Harrison illuminated me with flashes of meterological erudition. I only hope I didn't flood him with queries to graupel with.

'It's snowing still,' said Eeyore gloomily.
'So it is.'
'And freezing.'
'Is it?'
'Yes,' said Eeyore. 'However,' he said, brightening up a little, 'we haven't had an earthquake lately.'

A.A. Milne, *The House at Pooh Corner*